A MAP OF THE DARK

A Map of the Dark

John Dixon

Verse Chorus Press

Verse Chorus Press
PO Box 14806, Portland OR 97293
info@versechorus.com

The characters and events in this book are fictitious. Any similarity to real persons, living or dead, is coincidental and not intended by the author.

Cover art © Kate Wentz
Title page photograph © John Dixon
Book design by Steve Connell

FIRST EDITION

Printed in Canada

Library of Congress Cataloging-in-Publication Data

Dixon, John, 1952-
    A map of the dark / John Dixon.-- 1st ed.
    p. cm.
    Summary: "Relates a series of fictional events on Halloween 1963, in De Pere, Wisconsin, culminating in a murder"--Provided by publisher.
    ISBN 1-891241-21-4 (pbk.)
    1. De Pere (Wis.)--Fiction. 2. Halloween--Fiction. 3. Murder--Fiction. I. Title.
PS3604.I947M37 2005
813'.6--dc22
                                                    2005018751

For De Pere

1
CANDY LAND

Evelyn Schmidt got cancer in 1963. She found out the day before Halloween and was dead within a week. Halloween fell on a Thursday that year. It was the Halloween Chuck threw up, Carner went nuts, and Omsted's brother killed Putzie Van Vonderan.

During recess on Thursday morning Chuck found Omsted smoking a cigarette with Carner and Rusch in the corner of the church doorway. Omsted was saying, "—she's giving him a note this morning saying to meet her in Legion Park tonight at nine."

Rusch saw Chuck and said, "This doorway's only for sixth-graders."

Omsted said, "Leave him."

"He gives me the creeps hanging around all the time."

Omsted took the cigarette out of Rusch's hand, took a drag on it, and passed it to Carner. Carner stuck his head out of the doorway, looked around quickly, puffed on the cigarette, and passed it back to Rusch. Rusch took a drag off the cigarette and kept it.

Omsted punched Chuck on the shoulder.

Dale Lynkowski came around the corner chasing a kickball. Chuck slipped behind Omsted. Dale kicked the ball back towards the playground and ran off.

Rusch said, "My sister's got one of the Schmidt kids in her class."

Chuck said, "They ain't in class anymore. The nuns took 'em out."

"How do you know?"

"I got a friend—"

"Then why don't you go play with him?"

Rusch tried to hit Chuck on the back of the head. Chuck jumped out of the doorway and Rusch's hand hit the door instead. Carner and Omsted laughed. Rusch finished the cigarette, stepped on it, and said, "Let's get outta here."

On the way back to the playground Rusch asked Chuck if it was true he used to live in the house that Putzie Van Vonderan lived in.

"Might be."

"I sure wouldn't want a bunch of farmers living in my old house. They probably keep chickens in your old bedroom."

"I don't care if they keep Putzie in my old bedroom," Chuck said. "I don't sleep in it any more."

Rusch started to chase him, but Sister Fidelas came out of the school clanging the recess bell, yelling for everyone to get in line. Chuck ran to the line for the fifth grade; Rusch, Omsted, and Carner walked over to where the sixth-graders were lining up. When the fourth grade line went past on their way back inside, Dale Lynkowski asked Chuck why that bigger guy was chasing him.

Chuck said, "He wasn't chasing me. He's a friend of mine."

Sister Fidelas gave her bell a clang and yelled, "No talking in line!"

After lunch, Sister Brigitta, the principal, came around to each class and told them they should give up trick-or-treating that night and instead say a prayer for Evelyn's soul.

When school was over, Chuck cut out before Dale could find him and walked up the hill behind Omsted, Carner, and Rusch.

Rusch mimicked the way Sister Brigitta had talked about Evelyn. He gave Chuck a shove and said, "I bet you believed her, too."

Chuck said, "Nuns can't make up sins, only priests can."

Rusch poked Omsted and said, "See, I told you he was going trick-or-treating."

Chuck said, "I am not."

"Liar."

"What are you guys doing?"

"None of your business," Carner said.

They stopped at Erie Street to let a gas truck go past. Chuck said, "You're probably gonna wax the windows at the priest's house."

Rusch and Carner burst out laughing. Omsted turned around and winked at Chuck. They all crossed Erie Street.

Chuck said, "Last year me and Dale Lynkowski waxed the windows at the convent and they blamed David Schmidt."

"Waxing windows is for babies," Rusch said.

"It's probably better'n what you're doing."

Rusch stopped walking and turned to face Chuck.

Omsted said, "Don't even think about it."

Rusch started walking again, still facing Chuck. When Carner stopped at the corner, Rusch bumped into him.

Carner said "What?" and brushed his shoulder where Rusch had bumped him.

Omsted said, "Keep walking."

Rusch said, "Omsted's afraid I'm gonna spill the beans to the squirt."

Omsted said, "You ain't nuts" and crossed Huron Street with Carner.

Chuck tried to walk past Rusch, but Rusch caught him by the shoulder and said, "You wanna know what we're doing tonight?"

"I don't care what you're doing."

Omsted hollered across the street for Rusch to knock it off.

Rusch put his face close to Chuck's.

Carner and Omsted came back across Huron.

Rusch said, "We're going to Legion Park tonight. Omsted's brother is gonna kill Putzie Van Vonderan."

Omsted said, "Shit."

Rusch straightened up, smiling.

Chuck said, "So?"

Rusch's mouth fell open.

Carner hooted in a high, girlish voice.

Chuck said, "I don't care if he kills the whole family."

Omsted started laughing; then Carner, too. Rusch shoved Chuck backwards, called him a stupid little shit, and crossed Huron Street in front of a truck. The truck blew its horn, but Rusch gave it the finger and kept walking. Omsted sat down on a fire hydrant, laughing and holding his stomach.

After a while, Omsted said, "Squirt, you're all right" and the three of them continued walking. They caught up with Rusch at Ontario.

Ontario Street was where Legion Park started. It stretched five blocks up the hill and ended in a picnic grove at the top. The grove was full of oak trees, their yellow leaves on the ground. On the flat part below, elms had dropped red leaves onto the street. A tennis court took up the corner by Ontario, and behind it were a swing set and a shack that gave out bean bags in the summer. There was a mound of dead leaves against the shack where kids had made a leaf fort.

Across the street, on the corner, was the house where Evelyn Schmidt lived. It was a crumbling white house with a front hallway shaped like a church steeple, crooked steps down to the sidewalk, and a bare apple tree in the front yard.

When the boys reached Rusch he was standing with his arms folded, staring at the house. Carner bumped him in the back of the knees and said, "What you looking for? Ghosts?"

Rusch said, "You think she's still in there?"

Omsted said, "She's dying. They took her to the hospital."

"She ain't going to the hospital. She wants to die at home," Chuck said.

Rusch said, "How would you know?"

Chuck said, "My ma's friends with her."

Rusch and Carner and Omsted all looked at him.

"She was."

Rusch said, "I hope she ain't touched her lately."

"I didn't say she touched her. I said they were friends."

Rusch said, "I told you he was an idiot" and started down the block past Evelyn's house. Omsted and Carner followed, laughing. When Chuck tried to follow, Rusch turned around and shoved him. "Stay away from us, cancer boy."

Chuck fell on the sidewalk. He got up, wiping his hands on his jacket. "I don't have cancer."

Omsted told Rusch to knock it off.

A door banged in the backyard of a house a few doors down. A fat kid in an old coat threw a brown bag in a garbage can and ran back inside.

Rusch pointed through the yards and said, "There's your old house, asshole. Why don't you go back there and give Putzie's brother cancer?"

Then a door creaked and someone was coming out of Evelyn's house.

Carner screamed "Shit!" and ran into the middle of the road.

Rusch ran after him, waving his arms over his head, screaming, "It's Evelyn's ghost!"

Carner screamed again, like he meant it this time, and took off up the hill with Rusch behind him, still waving his arms. Omsted winked at Chuck and trotted off after the other two, picking up speed the closer he got to them.

The Schmidts' front door banged shut, and David's sister, Connie, was standing on the porch holding a jack-o'-lantern in her arms. She grinned at Chuck over the top of the jack-o'-lantern, but Chuck turned his head as though someone in the park was calling him and took off running towards the shack.

Halfway to the shack he cut up the hill, kicking up leaves as he ran into the picnic grove. He cut back to the road and came out of the park where the other guys should have been by now, but they were still a block below him, walking backwards, staring down the hill at Evelyn's house.

As Chuck came up behind them, Carner was saying, "He's probably in her house eating cookies."

Omsted said, "He ain't nuts."

Rusch said, "Let's clear out before he finds us again."

"I already found you," Chuck said.

They all jumped. Carner yelled, "Jesus Christ!" and wheeled around.

Rusch said, "She see you?"

"I think she chased me. I cut through the park."

Carner said, "She's dying. How could she chase you?"

"She ain't dead yet."

They walked up the hill, Carner ahead of the others. When a flock of geese flew over the park Carner stopped to watch them. Rusch collared him and spun him around to face Omsted and Chuck. Carner tried to shrug him off.

"Carner almost pissed his pants. I've never seen him so scared."

"I was scared because you were screaming."

Rusch messed up Carner's hair and let go of him. Carner yelled "goddamnit" and walked out into the road to comb his hair.

"Get a crew cut," Rusch said.

The others walked past Carner to Elm Street, the entrance to the subdivision where the nice houses started, houses with garages built into them and driveways in front instead of an alley in the back. By the time they reached Maple Street, where Chuck and Omsted lived, Carner had caught up with them. He and Rusch cut through a backyard to the street where the big houses were, the ones with yards like parks behind iron fences.

Chuck's house was on the first block of Maple Street. Omsted's was at the end of the second, where the road ended in a field of bare, black trees whose thick branches stretched across the sky. The sun was setting and the sky behind the trees was orange, then yellow, then green.

"God, I hate winter," Omsted said, looking up at the sky, his mouth tight.

Chuck said, "You think what Sister Brigitta said was true? About God remembering when it was our turn to die if we didn't give up trick-or-treating for Evelyn tonight?"

"By the time I'm ready to die, God ain't gonna remember who Evelyn was." They kept walking towards the black trees and the orange-green sky.

When they got to Chuck's house, Omsted stopped by the mailbox and said, "My brother's not really gonna kill Putzie Van Vonderan tonight."

"He's gonna beat him up though, ain't he?"

"He might."

"Did Putzie do something?"

"He's a farmer. He don't have to do nothing."

A crow cawed over their heads, disappeared among branches at the end of the road.

"He tried to say hello to my brother's girlfriend yesterday."

The crow cawed at them from the end of the block.

"It'd probably be better if you didn't tell anybody."

"What do I care if some farmer gets beat up?"

"You're all right, squirt." Omsted punched Chuck on the shoulder, said, "later," and took off at a run.

Chuck yelled, "What time are you going there?"

Omsted turned around, walking backwards, and said, "Late."

"I could go there with you."

"You got trick-or-treating to do."

"I ain't going."

"You better. Next year you'll be too old."

"I'm already—"

But Omsted yelled, "Save me some candy," and ran off down the block.

That night when Chuck came out of his room with his trick-or-treat bag his mother pushed her hair back with a handful of dishwater and asked why he wasn't wearing his pirate costume.

"It's in my bag," Chuck said. I'm putting it on at my friend's house."

Lizzie said, "He's lying. He doesn't have any friends." His sister was sitting at the kitchen table gluing pink sparkles to the back of her hands to match her princess dress.

Chuck said, "What are you gonna be? A Christmas cookie?"

Chuck's sister yelled to her mother that Chuck was making fun of her. Chuck said nobody needed to make fun of her, she was funny enough herself. Their mother told them both to shut up or they'd be doing their trick-or-treating in their rooms.

Chuck said, "I'm going," but his mother yelled, "Wait a minute" before he got to the back door.

Chuck waited, pushing the door open with his foot.

His mother pulled a plate out of the sink and rinsed it. His sister rubbed glue on her forehead, closed her eyes, and threw sprinkles in her face. His mother put her hands back in the dish water.

"Halloween's gonna be over in three hours, you know."

"Stay away from Ontario Street."

"I will."

Lizzie said, "He will not. He's going with Dale Lynkowski." She closed her eyes and shook some of the sprinkles off her face.

Chuck said, "She's spilling that stuff on the floor."

Chuck's mother turned her head, snapped at his sister that the house wasn't a pigsty, then turned back to Chuck.

"I promised Dale a long time ago."

"You shouldn't have."

"He has to go with Dale," Lizzie said. "All the guys up here think he's a baby."

Chuck said, "I'm going."

He went out the back door, kicking the storm door open so it would slam behind him. His mother caught it before it closed, and gave him a hard stare.

"What?" Chuck said.

"You stay away from David's house. His mother's sick."

"Like the whole town doesn't know that."

"And don't take any candy from him either."

"I know what cancer is."

In the kitchen, his sister said, "He swore." His mother turned and yelled at her to get the sparkles off the goddamn floor, and Chuck ran for the gate.

The moon was hiding at the edge of the sky when Chuck came out onto Maple Street. By the time he got to Legion Park it had climbed behind the trees, glowing orange, with clouds like black mountains behind it. At a white house with pillars across from the park, a fat guy in a tie was handing out candy to a crowd of kids. Chuck pulled his pirate mask out of his bag and ran up on the porch; the guy threw a purple Dum-Dum into his bag. Chuck ran back to the street, shoved his mask back in the bag, dug the Dum-Dum out, and walked down the hill sucking it.

A block further down, Rusch and Carner were waiting under a street light. Carner was holding onto a street sign with one hand, swinging around it in a slow circle. Rusch spotted Chuck and walked into the middle of the road to block his path. He pulled the Dum-Dum out of Chuck's mouth by the stick and said, "Look who's trick-or-treating."

"I am not."

Carner said, "Where'd you get the sucker then?"

"My ma's giving 'em out."

Carner came out into the road. "What about the trick-or-treat bag? She giving those out, too?"

Chuck said, "It's a present—for Evelyn."

Carner stepped behind Rusch.

Rusch said, "Bullshit."

Carner said, "You don't give presents to people with cancer."

A warm hand clamped itself around Chuck's mouth, and Omsted hollered, "You're dead!" He spun Chuck around and winked at him.

All three of the guys were wearing dark hooded sweatshirts.

Rusch said, "Don't touch him. He's got cancer."

Omsted said, "I touch you and you got cooties."

Carner said, "He's bringing that bag to Evelyn Schmidt."

"So? She ain't touched it yet." Omsted took his hand from Chuck's shoulder and wiped it on the front of his sweatshirt.

Something squealed in the dark, making Carner jump, and Spinelli slid to a stop on his bike. He was wearing a high-school letter jacket, red with white leather sleeves, and his blond hair was greased and combed into a curl over his forehead. He flicked his cigarette butt at Omsted's feet and asked, "Where's your brother?"

Rusch said, "Home practicing his swing."

Carner giggled.

Spinelli said, "Shut up, you two."

Rusch said, "Make me."

Spinelli said, "I don't make shit."

Omsted walked behind Spinelli's bike, snickering. He tapped his toe against Spinelli's back tire and said, "I hear Putzie almost wet his pants when your sister gave him that note this morning."

Spinelli said, "I asked you a question."

"I wasn't listening."

"Where the hell's your brother?"

Omsted shrugged and said, "Probably out looking for you."

"Shit." Spinelli shook his head at the group, spotted Chuck for the first time and said, "Who the hell are you?"

Chuck said, "Nobody you know."

"Good. Let's keep it that way," Spinelli said and stood up on the pedals of his bike.

Omsted said, "See you at the park."

"You stay the hell out of there," Spinelli said.

Rusch said, "It's a free park."

"Not tonight it ain't. You go near that park, you'll get your asses kicked." Spinelli slammed his feet down on the pedals, his back tire shot gravel, and he took off down the hill.

Rusch dived down by Omsted's feet and came up with Spinelli's cigarette. He shoved it in his mouth and drew hard, but it had already burned out. He tossed it back to the curb and said, "Let's get out of here."

Omsted waved over his shoulder and said, "Later, squirt."

"Where you guys going?"

Omsted said, "Out."

Rusch said, "And don't try to follow us or I'll kick your ass."

"I ain't afraid of you."

Rusch said, "You will be."

Carner giggled.

Omsted said, "You get any licorice, save it for me." He rapped his knuckles on Rusch's head, hollered that the last one down the hill was an asshole, and the three of them took off running. Halfway down the hill they started walking again, punching each other and laughing until they got to Ontario, then they ran screaming past Evelyn's house and disappeared in the dark under the trees near Erie Street.

Dale's house was next to Chuck's old house, on the same block as the Schmidts'. Chuck walked down the hill until he was almost to Ontario; then he ran past Evelyn's house and didn't stop until he got to Dale's. Dale was on the front steps in a superman costume, the mask tipped up on his head. A fat kid in a Spiderman costume was sitting on the steps behind him.

"Who's that?" Chuck asked.

The fat kid said, "I told ya he wouldn't recognize me."

He tipped his mask back. It was Putzie's brother, Little Lee.

"What's he doing here?"

Dale said, "My ma says we gotta ditch David."

Little Lee grinned and said, "So he asked me instead."

"Well, I'm unasking you." Chuck shoved him off the side of the steps. Lee fell on his back in the grass and cried out.

"Look, it's a talking blob."

Dale said, "Leave him alone."

Chuck put his mask on. "Anybody sees us, you tell 'em the farmer's with you."

Dale pulled his mask down over his face.

Little Lee said, "I live in the same house you used to."

Chuck said, "Yeah, but I moved when I heard the farmers were coming to town."

They skipped Little Lee's house because Chuck said he wasn't wasting his time on cheap farmer candy.

Little Lee said, "Banana chews ain't cheap."

"Maybe not to a farmer," Chuck said, and ran ahead of them to the Pflugers.

Mr. Pfluger was a beekeeper, so the Pflugers gave away Bit-O-Honeys every year. Chuck hollered, "Trick or treat," and when Little Lee and Dale came up on the porch behind him, Chuck stepped in front of Little Lee so it looked like Chuck and Dale were together and Little Lee was by himself. Mrs. Pfluger wore a black and yellow bonnet with antennas. She said any monsters that wanted treats from her were going to have to show their faces.

Chuck pushed up his mask and grinned.

Mrs. Pfluger dug a Bit-O-Honey out of her apron pocket and said it was good to see him in the neighborhood again. He thanked her and jumped off the porch.

When Little Lee lifted his mask she said, "I don't think I've seen you before." He told her he was Leroy Van Vonderan from the house next door. Mrs. Pfluger said, "That's right, the farm family," and gave him his candy bar.

On the sidewalk, Chuck told Little Lee to keep his mask down and if anyone asked who he was to say he was the mystery guest. Dale told Little Lee he could say whatever he wanted. Chuck said, "Remember that when the kids at school hear you been out trick-or-treating with farmers."

The house next to the Pflugers' was Evelyn's. Dale said they should cut across the street and go back up Ontario, but Chuck said if they ran past fast enough they could cut through Legion Park to the Kolbs' and nobody'd see them.

Little Lee said, "What if David's looking out the window?"

Chuck said, "We're wearing masks, stupid."

"He was with us when we bought 'em, stupid," Dale said.

Chuck said, "I ain't so stupid I hang out with farmers."

Little Lee yelled, "I ain't a farmer!"

Suddenly the Schmidts' front door creaked open; all three of them jumped behind the bushes next to the Pflugers' porch.

David came out of the house carrying a big white bowl, held the door open and set the bowl in front of it so it wouldn't close. The bowl was full of candy. David came to the bottom of the steps and stood there looking in the direction of Dale's house, his hand over his eyes. He kicked at the frozen grass for a minute, then went back in the house.

Dale said, "He's looking for us."

Little Lee said they should go before David came back.

Chuck told him to shut up.

Little Lee said, "It smells here."

"Yeah, like manure," Chuck said,

Dale whispered, "Shut up," and clamped his hand over Little Lee's mouth as David came back out carrying a jack-o'-lantern so big he couldn't get his arms all the way around it. He dropped the jack-o'-lantern against the door next to the bowl and came back down to the sidewalk, looking up and down the street this time. He was wearing long underwear dyed red and had a devil's mask tipped back on his head. His sister came out of the house in beat-up yellow pajamas, a mouse mask around her neck. She took a piece of candy from the bowl, unwrapped it and ate it. David came back to the steps and sat at the bottom with his back to her.

Laughter broke out in the dark. David looked up. Connie scrambled down the steps and past him to the sidewalk. A big girl ran out of the park chasing a smaller girl; both were wearing duck masks. They ran past Connie, giggling, and on to the Pflugers' porch, hollering "Trick or treat!" and collapsing against one another. Connie came back to the steps.

David said, "Your friends ain't coming."

Connie said, "Neither are Chuck and Dale."

"Chuck and Dale ain't babies."

"They're assholes."

"You don't even know what an asshole is."

Connie climbed past David and sat down next to the candy. The ducks left the Pflugers' and ran off down Ontario Street, passing Aunt Jemima and the president's wife coming from Little Lee's. The president's wife saw David and poked Aunt Jemima. Aunt Jemima threw her hands up and screamed. They ran past David and Connie and vanished into the park.

Little Lee pulled Dale's hand off his mouth and said, "I ain't spending Halloween under a porch."

Chuck muttered, "Why not? You probably spent last Halloween in a barn."

Little Lee raised his voice, "I did not—" but Dale clamped his hand so tight around his mouth that Little Lee gagged.

Dale whispered, "Shut up or I'll rip your tongue out!"

Little Lee's eyes got wide behind Dale's hand. He nodded his head up and down fast. Dale rook his hand away. Little Lee started to whisper he wouldn't do it again, then there was another noise on the Schmidts' porch and they all turned to look.

"Holy cripes," Chuck whispered.

Evelyn was standing on the porch in a purple house dress, her hair in pin curls, a cigarette dangling from her lips. Loose skin hung from her arms, and her legs were like sticks. She said to her kids, "Where are your friends?"

David said, "What do you care?" He was staring through the railing at the Pflugers' bushes.

"Don't you play smart-ass with me. I'm not in the mood," Evelyn said and undid one of her pin curls. She ran the hair between her fingers, then nudged the candy bowl with her foot and said, "If you're going to sit there, you can hand out candy while I take down my hair."

David said, "Nobody wants our candy."

"And I suppose that's my fault."

David turned to look up at her, his mouth hanging open.

Two little ghosts and a pumpkin-head came running out of the park. Evelyn reached down for the candy bowl.

"Don't," David said.

Evelyn picked her way down the steps between Connie and David, the candy bowl shaking in her hands, and reached the sidewalk as the ghosts and the pumpkin-head ran across the street.

She took a handful of candy from the bowl and held it out to them.

The ghosts and the pumpkin-head froze when they saw Evelyn blocking their path. She raised the handful of candy, and when they didn't move to take it she said "Happy Halloween" in a shaky voice. The pumpkin-head screamed, then the ghosts screamed, and all three ran out into the street, past Evelyn, past the Pflugers', and disappeared into the darkness.

A skeleton coming in the opposite direction saw Evelyn, shrieked, and ran into the park.

David ran out to the sidewalk and yelled, "You pig, Neumeyer!" after the skeleton. The skeleton shrieked again in the darkness. The candy in Evelyn's hand fell to the sidewalk. David knelt and scooped the candy into a pile.

Evelyn said, "It's okay."

"It is not okay!"

She reached down to put a hand on his shoulder and grabbed him by the collar when he tried to break away. She staggered as he jerked and turned, but held him tight by the back of his costume, the candy bowl tucked under her other arm. She shook him and yelled, "Listen to me."

David stopped struggling.

"I want you to take your sister and go trick-or-treating."

Connie yelled from the porch that she was waiting for Linda and Jane.

"I want you to go with your brother. Go get your bags."

Connie got up and stomped into the house.

"I ain't going," David said.

"I need you to take Connie. She can't go on her own."

"Then why don't you stay home and take her instead of getting drunk?"

Evelyn flung him away from her and he fell backward against a tree.

"I don't want none of your games tonight, buster. You take your sister and you go trick-or-treating, and if she comes home crying you'll *wish* I was drunk."

David began to snivel. His mother went back up the steps and into the house, banging the candy dish down next to the door.

Chuck whispered, "What a crybaby."

Little Lee said, "She could've hurt him when she slammed him into that tree."

Connie came out with two grocery bags with pumpkins drawn on them, her mouse mask over her face. She stood by the tree next to David, holding one of the bags out to him.

David turned his face away.

Connie cried, "Mom said!" from under her mask.

David stood up, grabbed the bag, and marched out of the yard with Connie running after him.

Chuck jabbed Dale in the back and said, "Let's get out of here."

They climbed out from behind the Pflugers' bushes and ran down Ontario Street, not stopping till they got to Dale's house. Little Lee was out of breath and the front of his costume was stained with sweat.

Chuck said, "If you weren't so fat, you could run faster."

"He ain't fat," Dale said.

"Tell me that ain't blubber hanging out from under his mask."

There was screaming nearby. Little Lee jumped behind Dale. Omsted, Rusch, and Carner came running down the middle of the road, hoods pulled up, grabbing eggs from their sweatshirt pouches and throwing them at a couple of passing cars. They disappeared down George Street, heading for downtown.

Chuck said, "Let's work our way down to the stores. We'll get really good stuff if we get to Red Owl before it closes."

Little Lee said his mother didn't want him to go downtown.

Chuck said, "Good. You can trick-or-treat on this block and me and Dale can go by ourselves."

Dale said, "We can work our way up the hill. People up there were giving out caramel apples and stuff last year."

They walked to the corner of George and Ontario. A few blocks down, where the lights of the stores started, the guys were still hollering in the middle of the street.

Chuck said, "Ford's Grocery is probably giving out candy bars." He turned down George, nodding at Dale over his shoulder to follow him.

Dale said, "The Huevelmans are probably giving out Slo Pokes again. Last year they ran out before we got there." He turned up George towards the hill.

Little Lee said, "What's a Slo Poke?"

"Like you only not so fat," Chuck said.

Dale headed away from Chuck up George Street. Little Lee raised his mask to stick his tongue out at Chuck, then followed Dale. Chuck watched until they were almost to the first house then ran to catch up to them. He elbowed Little Lee in the side as he went past.

Little Lee said, "Ouch."

Chuck said, "Watch where you're going," then cut in front of Little Lee to walk next to Dale and said, "After the Huevelmans' I'm going downtown whether anyone else comes or not."

The first house had all its lights off. The second house was where Mr. Cotter, the undertaker, lived; nobody went there. The third house was Mrs. Beno's. She gave out candy kisses. Chuck tried to trip Little Lee going up the steps, but missed and tripped a first-grader instead. When they were back on the sidewalk Chuck said, "Your farmer friend tripped that kid and almost killed him."

"He's not a farmer," Dale said.

Little Lee swallowed the candy kiss he was eating, but before he could speak Chuck said, "Let's cut across and see if the Gerkes are giving out popcorn balls again."

They ran across to the Gerkes', then back to the Hagers', then down to the Danens' on the corner. The Gerkes had popcorn balls, the Hagers gave out Tootsie Rolls, and the Danens had candy corn. On Huron Street they got candy corn at three more houses, and the Lietermans gave them Baby Ruths.

There were kids running everywhere by now, and people just stood in their doorways, handing out candy as the kids ran up. There was a crowd at the Huevelmans'. Chuck took his mask off and went through the line a second time. When he got back to the sidewalk, Little Lee told him going through the line twice was a sin.

"So go tell a nun," Chuck said.

Little Lee peeled the wrapper off his Slo Poke and took a bite.

"No wonder you're so fat."

"You're *supposed* to eat candy on Halloween."

"Not all of it."

Dale said he was going to the Johnsons' and cut across the street. Little Lee followed, his mask tipped back on his head and the Slo Poke sticking out of his mouth. By the time Chuck crossed the street, Dale and Little Lee were already on the porch with a bunch of other kids. Mrs. Johnson, dressed like a witch, yanked the door open and cackled, "Who wants my ginger snaps?"

Chuck ducked behind a tree at the curb. Dale tried to jump off the porch but Mrs. Johnson collared him, saying, "Not so fast, little boy," and led him into the house with the rest of the giggling kids. Mr. Johnson, dressed as Frankenstein, pulled the door shut.

Chuck ran back across the street and trick-or-treated his way down the block. He got home-made fudge, Dum-Dums, and a Clark Bar. He heard more screaming from downtown and saw guys running in and out of traffic by the school, but before he could tell who they were they ran off down a side street. He worked his way back to the Johnsons', getting there just as Dale and the other kids came running out to the sidewalk. Mrs. Johnson was still cackling on the porch behind them.

Chuck said, "You stupids."

Dale said, "She made us eat cookies."

Little Lee said, "She tried to make us drink toad soup."

Dale said, "It was apple juice."

"Like a farmer'd know the difference," Chuck said.

Dale scanned the other side of the street and said, "I think I'll go see what the Vandeheys are giving out."

Chuck said, "I was already there. They're giving out cookies, too."

Dale said, "What about the Hansens', and the house on the corner?"

"Cookies."

"What kind of cookies?" Little Lee said.

Dale said, "Who cares?" and started down the street towards the park.

"I thought we were going downtown," Chuck said.

Dale kept walking. "We can cut through the park to the Kolbs'. The houses are closer together there."

Little Lee stuck to Dale's side. He asked if they shouldn't be scared to walk through the park at night. Chuck waited until they'd crossed the street before running to catch up with them.

It was windy in the park, and the street lights creaked on their wires, making shadows that reached down from the trees. The moon was behind the clouds by now, gleaming high and white. Little Lee pointed up at it and said it was creepy.

Chuck came up behind them and said, "So go back home if you're scared."

"I didn't say I was scared. I said it was creepy."

"What's the difference?"

"You're creepy and I'm not afraid of you," Little Lee said.

Dale laughed.

Chuck shoved Little Lee into a pile of leaves and kneeled on his chest. He tore Lee's mask off and yelled, "You afraid of me now, farmer?"

Lee shouted for Dale. Dale put his hand on Chuck's shoulder. Chuck shrugged him off. He grabbed a handful of leaves and shoved them in Lee's face. "I asked, are you afraid of me now!"

Little Lee spat and choked on the leaves. Dale put his hand back on Chuck's shoulder, and when Chuck tried to shrug him off again, Dale shoved back hard, knocking Chuck into the grass. Chuck scrambled to his feet, facing Dale over Little Lee, who lay on his back squealing.

Dale yelled at Little Lee to get up.

Chuck said, "He can't get up. He's too fat."

"Nobody's asking you," Dale shouted. He picked Little Lee's mask up from the grass. Broken elastic dangled from one side.

Chuck said. "I ain't going trick-or-treating with anybody that ain't got a mask."

Little Lee pushed himself to his knees, yelling, "You broke it, asshole!"

Chuck went after Lee, hollering, "What did you call me, you farmer?"

"You're an asshole!"

"Both of you shut up," Dale said. He stepped between them,

putting a hand out to protect Little Lee.

Chuck yelled, "I don't gotta take lip from farmers" and tried to break past Dale, but Dale backhanded him, catching him right in the mouth.

Chuck stepped backwards and shook his head. His face stung and his ears were ringing. Dale held his ground, his eyes on Chuck. Little Lee was on his feet now, shaky hands twisting the top of his bag into a knot.

Chuck dragged his feet through the leaves over to a picnic table and sat on it.

Dale tied the elastic back on to Lee's Spiderman mask and handed it to him.

Chuck said, "What are you now? His maid?"

"At least I ain't an asshole."

"I'd rather be an asshole than a farmer's friend."

Little Lee put on his mask and pushed it up to the top of his head. He and Dale headed out of the park without looking back at Chuck.

Chuck watched them until they got to the tennis court then hollered, "Don't worry about that mask breaking again. You can always go as a farmer and scare people to death."

He dug a handful of candy corn out of his bag and ate it one piece at a time as he watched the two of them leave the park. When they disappeared into the crowd, he folded his bag under his arm and followed.

There were lots of kids on the street , running down the sidewalks and up onto porches, jumping off porches and cutting across yards. Most of the houses had jack-o'-lanterns on their steps or ghosts in their trees. One house had a trellis with bats hanging from it. Chuck spotted Dale and Little Lee on the porch of a house with cobwebs in the windows. He went on to the next one.

When they caught up with him at the third house he cut across the street. He passed them at the corner, crossing to the opposite side. Dale glared at him like he wanted to say something and Little Lee stuck his tongue out just as they went past. Chuck picked up a rock from the road and tossed it at Little Lee's head, but it missed and hit Wilma Flintstone in the back.

There was more screaming down by the school and a group of bigger kids ran out into George Street carrying a jack-o'-lantern over their heads. They were close enough for Chuck to see their hoods and he could almost make out Omsted's face. Chuck tucked his mask under his arm and ran to catch up with them, but before he even reached Huron Street they'd smashed the pumpkin on the roof of a passing car and disappeared back into the dark.

Chuck put his mask back on and turned down Huron. Kids were moving in mobs by now and Chuck was trick-or-treating at the same house as Dale and Little Lee before he noticed he'd caught up with them. They were in line ahead of him and he thought about jumping off the porch, but it looked like they were getting Snickers bars so he stayed. Little Lee stuck his nose in the air as he went past and almost fell down the steps. Dale stared Chuck down, then nodded at the last minute. Chuck laughed in his face.

Chuck cut over to Erie, but after three houses he ran into them again. It was an old house with a big porch and no railing. As Chuck was leaving he elbowed Little Lee in the side and knocked him off the porch. Lee fell into the bushes and screamed.

Chuck said, "Stupid farmers can't even walk straight."

A kid on the porch laughed and another kid mooed.

The guy handing out candy said, "That's enough of that."

Chuck oinked and jumped off the porch, landing in the front yard in time to see Omsted, Rusch, and Carner run down George

Street with a leaf dummy on their backs.

Chuck dashed to the corner. There were trick-or-treaters down by the stores, and the leaf dummy was lying in the road between the church and the Texaco station, but the guys were already gone. A car full of Draculas ran over the dummy; it exploded and the Draculas laughed.

Chuck headed downtown.

The first store on George Street was Ford's Grocery. Little Lee and Dale were standing outside the building in the dark just off George. Lee's hands were shaking again. Dale grabbed Lee by the front of his costume and pulled him into the light from the store just as Chuck came across the street. They saw Chuck and froze.

Dale nodded at Chuck again. This time Chuck stared back, but smiled like he was thinking of a joke. He didn't take his eyes off Dale until he'd stepped up onto the curb in front of him.

A beat-up station wagon jerked to a stop in front of the grocery, banging and shooting out smoke. Lee saw the station wagon, let out a cry, and ran off into the dark down Superior Street.

Dale yelled, "Little Lee!"

Chuck pointed down Superior and laughed.

The back door of the station wagon opened, and a pile of kids wearing paper-bag masks fell out. A tall kid in a white shirt with a Frankenstein bag on his head lifted out a little girl in a pink dress and a bag made into a crown through the front window. The other kids, all around Chuck's age, spilled out of the back door until the sidewalk was full. The skinny guy at the wheel told the kids he'd meet them at the end of the block.

The tall kid said, "We wanna go to the drugstore."

The guy hollered, "The end of the block!" and drove off.

The little girl in the pink dress grabbed the tall kid by the hand

and the whole gang followed her into Ford's.

There was a crash inside the store and the kids in the paper-bag masks ran back out. Somebody laughed inside and somebody swore; the door flew open and Omsted, Carner, and Rusch ran out, old man Ford chasing them. He got tangled up with the kids on the sidewalk, and by the time he got free Omsted and the other guys were already at the end of the block. Old man Ford shook his fist and yelled, "I know your names, you little bastards!"

The tall kid put his hands over the little girl's ears; the other kids giggled.

Rusch yelled, "We know yours, too, asshole!" and the three of them ran down a side street by the dentist's office.

Old man Ford cursed and went back into the store. The kids from the station wagon piled in after him. Chuck and Dale went in last and elbowed their way to the front. Casey Ford, the old man's son, was sitting on the counter dressed as a vampire with red lipstick on his neck for blood and a plastic pumpkin filled with candy on his lap. The candy rack behind the counter had been tipped over and there was candy all over the floor.

Old man Ford yelled at the kids not to step on anything. Then he yelled at Casey, "Are you just going to sit there and let hooligans take over the entire store?"

Casey banged the pumpkin down on the counter and stormed into the back room, slamming the door behind him.

Old man Ford looked at the kids, the floor, and the broken rack behind the counter. He pointed to the pumpkin and said, "Each of you take one piece of candy and get out of here."

The kids crowded around the pumpkin. Old man Ford yelled at them not to step on the candy on the floor unless they meant to pay for it; then he started kicking the candy into piles. There was a Slo Poke on the floor next to Chuck. He kicked it away from the rest of the candy and it slid across the floor and hit Dale's foot.

Old man Ford yelled, "I saw that."

Dale said, "I didn't do nothing."

"He didn't," Chuck said. "I saw him. It was that guy there."

Chuck pointed at the tall guy in the Frankenstein mask.

The tall kid said, "That's a lie!"

He was holding a Tootsie Roll he'd taken from the pumpkin. Old man Ford grabbed his hand, pulled the Tootsie Roll out of it and threw it back in the pumpkin.

The tall kid shouted, "That's not fair!"

Old man Ford said, "I'll give you fair. You're too damn old to be trick-or-treating anyway."

The tall kid stared at old man Ford, breathing hard through his mask, then turned and went outside.

Old man Ford said, "The rest of you get your candy and get out of here."

Casey came out of the back room wearing a white T-shirt, the blood washed off his neck. He pulled on his letter jacket and left the store without looking back. While old man Ford was watching Casey, Chuck grabbed two handfuls of candy from the pumpkin and walked out.

Outside, the tall guy had taken off his mask and was smoking a cigarette. He had big ears and a pimply face. The girl in the pink dress dug a sucker out of her bag and offered it to him, but the tall guy shook his head. Dale was in the doorway eating a Dum-Dum. When he saw Chuck, the tall guy threw his cigarette down and began to lead the other kids away.

Dale nodded at Chuck.

Chuck said, "You lost Little Lee?"

The girl in the pink dress turned and said, "Little Lee?" She came running back up the block, calling out, "Little Lee's here!"

When she got to Chuck she said, "Where's Little Lee?"

Chuck said, "He's dead."

The tall kid hollered, "Deena, get back here."

The little girl's lip started to shake.

"A cow ate him," Chuck said.

The girl started bawling and ran back down the block towards the others. The tall kid came to meet her, picked her up, and carried her to the corner where the skinny guy was waiting in the station wagon.

Dale stared at Chuck and rolled the Dum-Dum around in his mouth.

Chuck said, "So where's your friend?"

Dale said, "I guess he's afraid of stores."

Two small mice ran past them into the store. Old man Ford yelled, "We're closed! Get the hell out!" and they ran off screaming down the block.

Chuck said, "I bet the drugstore's giving out chocolate pumpkins again."

Dale said, "You want to go see?"

Chuck shrugged. They began walking together down the block.

Danen's Bakery was closed; so was Hansen's Hardware. The dummies in the dress shop window were all wearing Lone Ranger masks and funny hats, but the store was closed. The dentist's office was open and so was the De Pere Theater. Kids were running back and forth across the street between them.

The station wagon went by. The little girl was sitting on the tall kid's lap. The guy who was driving pointed his finger across the seat at the tall guy and yelled at him.

Chuck asked Dale if he wanted to see what the theater was giving out.

Dale said, "It's probably Jujubes."

"It might be popcorn," Chuck said, and dodged between the cars over to the theater. Dale followed. They got Milk Duds, then ran back across the street to the drugstore.

There was a party at the bar next to the drugstore on the corner. They had a jack-o'-lantern in the window and leaf dummies with beer bottles hanging by their necks on either side of it. A song about dancing monsters blared out through the doorway.

A woman in a swimsuit ran out of the bar with a champagne glass in her hand. When she saw Chuck and Dale she screamed, "Oh my God, monsters!" and ran back inside.

A woman inside the bar shouted, "Happy New Year!"

Chuck said, "You think they're giving anything?"

Dale said, "Probably cigarettes."

"Maybe beer." Chuck cupped his hands to the window to try and see inside.

"I wonder if Evelyn's in there?"

Dale said, "She's dying. They wouldn't let her in."

The woman in the swimsuit pointed out the door and screamed, "Monsters! Monsters!" Chuck and Dale ran around the corner to the drugstore.

Little Lee was waiting outside the drugstore, holding his candy bag with both hands. It was torn at the top from where he'd been twisting it, and the bottom was starting to show holes.

Dale asked him why he didn't wait outside Ford's.

Little Lee said, "I took a short cut."

Chuck said, "It must have been a farmer's shortcut—five times around the block."

"I got here before you did," Little Lee said.

Chuck started into the drugstore, then stopped, his hand on the door.

Little Lee said, "You gotta open the door to get in, you know."

Omsted, Carner, and Rusch were standing at the register with their arms folded. Mr. Giese was behind the counter shaking his head. Chuck moved back from the door and said, "Go in, if you're in such a hurry."

"I will." Little Lee turned his nose up at Chuck and went inside. Dale looked at Chuck then followed Little Lee. Chuck took his mask off, put it in his bag, and hid his bag in the doorway of the doctor's office next door. Then he counted to ten and went into the drugstore.

Omsted was leaning over the counter towards Mr. Giese, Carner and Rusch tight behind him. Dale and Little Lee were whispering by the postcard rack.

Omsted was saying, "This is my Halloween costume. I'm Elvis's brother."

Mr. Giese said, "I don't care if you're Elvis's sister. Get out of my store."

Carner looked round as Chuck came into the store and said, "Here's Elvis's dead baby. What does he get?"

"A ride to the police station with the rest of you in about fifteen seconds," Mr. Giese said.

Chuck came down the aisle past Dale and Little Lee and stopped at the counter behind Omsted and the other guys.

Little Lee whispered, "Where's your mask?"

"I'm wearing it," Chuck said.

Dale took Little Lee by the arm and said, "Let's get outta here."

Omsted said, "Hey, squirt."

Rusch said, "I thought you weren't trick-or-treating."

"I'm not. I came in to rob the place."

Dale dragged Little Lee a few steps backward.

Omsted and Rusch and Carner laughed.

Mr. Giese leaned over the counter and yelled, "You *what!*"

The older boys looked at the younger boys. Little Lee looked at the floor. Chuck grinned at Omsted.

"You came in to *what?*"

Little Lee looked up and said, "Trick or treat?"

Carner laughed.

Rusch roared.

Chuck stepped up beside Omsted and said, "Trick or treat my ass."

Omsted clapped Chuck on the back.

Mr. Giese said, "That's it," pulled a telephone from under the register, and put the receiver to his ear. Before he could dial, Chuck reached over the counter and knocked a rack of gum to the floor. Omsted whooped, Rusch howled. Carner grabbed a handful of gum and ran out the door, knocking Little Lee into the postcard rack. Mr. Giese tried to dial but he was watching the boys and his fingers kept missing the holes. Omsted and Rusch grabbed handfuls of gum. Chuck made a grab for a candy bar but Giese dropped the phone and grabbed him by the arm.

"Let me go, you fuck!" Chuck yelled.

Mr. Giese' mouth fell open and he let go of Chuck's arm. Omsted grabbed Chuck by the back of his jacket, spun him around and pushed him towards the front of the store, knocking over Dale who was trying to pull Little Lee out of the broken postcard rack.

Rusch and Carner were hiding in the doorway of the doctor's office. They jumped out screaming when Omsted and Chuck ran past. Rusch had Chuck's candy bag. It was torn open, and Chuck's pirate mask was smashed on the ground. Rusch was stuffing the candy into the pouch of his sweatshirt.

Omsted slapped Chuck on the back, yelling, "Trick or treat my ass!"

The door to the drugstore flew open. Dale and Little Lee stumbled out, and the door banged shut behind them. They stood together on the sidewalk, glaring at Chuck. Carner and Rusch stopped laughing.

Chuck said, "What are you looking at?"

Dale said, "He called the cops."

Omsted said, "The cops don't even know who he is."

Little Lee said, "I know who he is."

Omsted said, "Then if the cops find out it's gonna be your problem, ain't it?"

Little Lee ducked behind Dale. His hands began to shake.

Dale said, "We're going."

Chuck said, "Be sure you take cowface with you."

"I'm not a cowface!" Little Lee yelled. His bag rattled, and his head and shoulders began to shake, too.

Rusch said, "What's wrong with him?"

"He's Putzie's brother," Chuck said.

Carner said, "It figures."

Rusch said, "He's as ugly as his brother, too."

"My brother ain't ugly," Little Lee said.

Chuck said, "Your brother's a retard."

"Ignore him," Dale said and began to drag Little Lee across the street.

Little Lee pulled away and yelled at Chuck, "He ain't too retarded to beat you up!"

"Your brother ain't beating up anybody—"

Carner hollered, "Danger! Danger!"

"My brother can pound you all to pulp!"

"Your brother ain't making anybody into pulp! Your brother's gonna *be* pulp!"

Omsted said, "Squirt—" and grabbed for Chuck's shoulder.

"Omsted's brother's gonna kill him in Legion Park tonight!" Chuck yelled.

Everybody froze.

Rusch hollered, "Shit!"

Little Lee shouted, "You're a liar!"

Rusch lunged at Chuck, but Omsted had already pushed him hard against the drugstore window and was holding him by the throat.

Lee shook so hard that candy flew out of his bag.

Mr. Giese yelled, "I called the police!" The lights in front of the drugstore went off.

"Tell him it was a joke," Omsted hissed at Chuck.

Chuck made a gasping noise and pulled at Omsted's hand on his throat.

"You're coming over there with me and telling your little friend you were making a bad joke."

Omsted spun Chuck around, grabbed him by the collar, and marched him over to Little Lee. Rusch and Carner followed close behind. Little Lee dropped his candy bag, covered his head with his arms, and shouted, "Leave me alone!"

Omsted said, "Your friend wants to talk to you."

Dale moved closer to Little Lee and said, "He ain't our friend."

"You're gonna listen anyway," Rusch said.

He pushed Dale off the curb, grabbed Little Lee by the neck and pried his arms away from his head. Little Lee screamed. Carner went out to the curb and looked up and down the street.

Rusch clamped his hands on Little Lee's shoulders and said, "Shut up. Nobody's hurting you."

Little Lee stopped screaming and started to sniffle.

Omsted said, "Squirt's got something he wants to tell you." He shook Chuck by the neck.

Chuck said, "It was a joke."

Omsted said, "And—" He gave Chuck another shake.

Chuck said, "I just made it up to scare you."

Lee said, "I'm telling my mom."

"No, you're not," Rusch said.

A cop siren flared up a few blocks away. Carner ran back from the curb, "Christ, it's the cops! He really called them."

Omsted took his hand off Chuck's neck and said, "Everybody walk nice and normal around the corner."

They all started walking, Rusch in front with Dale and Little Lee, Carner and Omsted behind them with Chuck. The siren wailed closer.

Rusch put his hand on Dale's shoulder and said, "What's your name?"

Dale said, "None of your business."

"You think I can't find out?"

"Go to hell."

Rusch tightened his grip on Dale's shoulder and said, "You tell your farmer friend to shut up about his brother or I'll find out who you are and kick every one of your teeth down your fucking throat."

They turned the corner by the drugstore and Omsted hollered, "Run!"

Dale dashed across the street, Little Lee whining behind him, and disappeared down the alley next to the theater. Carner and Rusch cut into the alley between the bar and the post office. Carner whined, "Oh, Jesus Christ!" as the siren wailed closer. Chuck was headed past the post office when a hand grabbed him from behind and sent him flying down the alley behind Carner and Rusch.

"Under the truck," Omsted said and pushed Chuck towards a cement truck where Rusch and Carner were already hiding. Chuck slid in next to Rusch, who whacked him on the back of the head as Omsted dived under the truck.

They lay flat on their stomachs and buried their heads in their arms as the cop car drove past, flashed a light down the alley, and went on.

None of them moved. They could hear people screaming a couple of blocks away and the cop car driving up George Street. Then Omsted started to laugh.

Carner said, "It wouldn't be so funny if they caught us."

"We'd be the first people ever got caught by the De Pere police," Omsted said.

Rusch slapped Carner on the shoulder and said, "Carner's been afraid of the cops ever since he heard the De Pere jail had spiders in it."

Omsted said, "Hell, there's worse than that under this truck."

Carner scurried out from under the truck, kicking up gravel. The others crawled out after him, laughing at Carner as they slapped dust off their clothes.

Rusch nodded at Chuck and said, "So we gonna kill this little son of a bitch or what?"

"We're taking him with us," Omsted said.

"Are you nuts? He already ratted us out once."

"And if he's with us, we can keep him from doing it twice."

Carner said, "That's just rewarding him for being a moron."

"And you've never said anything you weren't supposed to?" Rusch said, "I haven't."

"You're the one who told me about Putzie," Chuck said.

It was dead quiet for a moment, then Omsted laughed, a cackling laugh that got louder when Rusch glared at him.

Rusch said, "Are we gonna do something while the stores are still open or what?"

Omsted clapped Chuck on the shoulder and said, "Let's hit the dime store and show the squirt how to steal cigarettes from Fat Man Durant."

"Maybe Durant'll have a gun and we can get the little asshole shot," Rusch said and headed out of the alley. Carner caught up with him, combing his hair as they walked.

Omsted asked Chuck if he'd ever stolen anything before.

"Lots of stuff."

"Good. We can go steal more eggs when we're done at Durant's." Omsted slapped Chuck on the back and they ran out of the alley, catching up with Carner and Rusch as they reached the street. Rusch hollered like an Indian. Carner screamed like a girl. A car full of skeletons drove by and screamed back at him.

A man in a white shirt came out of the bar and yelled, "You boys are being a nuisance!"

"It's Halloween, asshole. We can be anything we want!" Chuck yelled back.

He turned and ran after Omsted, dodging traffic, howling at the smaller kids, and laughing all the way to the dime store.

2
ODD GIRL OUT

Two angels ran giggling past Evelyn into Ford's grocery and a scarecrow ran out and headed downtown. A little girl with a daisy for a head peeked out from the open doorway, saw Evelyn, and dashed out to the sidewalk, holding up a tiny red bucket of candy and smiling.

Evelyn said, "Aren't you pretty?" and bent her face close to the girl's.

The girl pushed her bucket against Evelyn's coat and said, "Treat."

Evelyn opened her purse. The girl giggled and put her hand in her mouth. A woman came out of the store, saw Evelyn, and hollered, "Kathy Kasmerick! Get back here now!"

The girl ran back to the doorway. The woman caught her by the hair, jabbed a knee into her back and yelled, "Don't you *ever* run off like that!" The woman pushed the bawling girl inside and glared at Evelyn, then turned back into the store.

Evelyn closed her purse and hurried past the grocery door. The woman inside dumped the girl's candy bucket onto the counter, shouting, "What did she give you?"

Ed Ford pushed the door shut and turned out the light on his grocery sign.

The wind spun down George Street, slapping candy wrappers against her legs and blowing clouds over the moon. A devil ran out from behind the hardware store, waved his pitchfork at her, ran screaming across the street and disappeared behind the gas station. Evelyn put her head down, pulled her coat tight around her neck, and fought her way through the wind to the Idle Hour.

The Idle Hour was a glow in the dark at the end of George with a jack-o'-lantern in the window and a rock-and-roll song blaring from the doorway.

Dale Lynkowski and Chuck Williams stood in front of the window, their faces pressed to the glass. Vera Muller stumbled out of the bar in a swimsuit, shouted "Monsters! Monsters!" and the boys ran off down the block.

Evelyn came out of the dark, taking off her kerchief and shaking out her hair. "Don't we look lovely this evening?" she said.

Vera jumped. Her mouth fell open and her fat hand flew to her throat. She turned and ran back into the bar.

The top half of the door was open. Curls of crepe paper were draped across the corners. The bottom had a picture of a black cat taped to it. The song on the jukebox ended. Men laughed; then they stopped. Vera said, "Don't everybody look—" as Evelyn pushed the bottom half-door open and stepped into the bar.

Black crepe hung in loops from the ceiling and was tied in knots like spider webs on the walls. The pool table had been pushed into a corner to make room for a dance floor in front of the jukebox, with three tables and some chairs arranged in a half circle around it. Vera was at the middle table, wearing a plastic crown, hunched over her drink. Rolls of fat stuck out between her arms and the straps of her suit. Her husband Jerry sprawled next to her, his feet on a chair, and stared at Evelyn over the top of his beer bottle. There were maybe a dozen people in the bar, and all of them were looking at Evelyn.

In the corner near the door, Cy Omsted was hanging over Betty Vandehey. Betty was a devil in a shiny red dress, holding a tiny red pitchfork. Cy was the Lone Ranger, standing behind Betty's stool with his mouth on her ear and his eyes on Evelyn. There was an empty stool next to Betty. When Evelyn looked at it, Betty put her pitchfork on the stool, nudged Cy and said, "Sit down, for God's sake."

Cy unwrapped himself from Betty, picked up the pitchfork and sat on the stool. Halfway down the bar, Barney the bartender rapped his hand on the counter and hollered, "Down here, beautiful. I'm keeping a stool warm for you."

Evelyn walked down toward Barney, past Smokey DeWitt, grinning at her with horns sticking out of his head, past a drunk she'd never seen before, past Alice DeGroot, whose forehead was slowly sinking down over her beer bottle. There were three empty stools next to Alice. Beyond them, Rudi Erickson stood over his drink and looked down at Evelyn. He turned away as Evelyn smiled and said something to a little guy in a blue suit, who said, "No!" and stuck his head around Rudi to look at her.

Barney set a glass of beer halfway between Alice and Rudi. When Evelyn pulled herself up onto the stool across from it, Rudi slid his drink towards the little guy. There was a scraping of stools all the way down the bar.

Evelyn slid a quarter across the counter, but Barney slid it back. "It's Halloween. The first one's on me."

Evelyn said, "Isn't that lovely?" and raised her glass to him. She tipped her head back and took a long swallow.

Barney ran a finger under the collar of his white shirt, pulling at the button behind his bow tie, watching Evelyn drink. When she set her glass down it was half empty. She smiled at Barney. He took his finger from under his collar and said, "I'm surprised you made it in tonight."

Evelyn said, "Why?"

"Oh, hell . . . I don't know." Barney looked down at the floor, then up and down the bar as if someone was calling him. Betty raised her hand and he hurried down to her, wiping his hands on the bar rag tucked in his belt.

Betty leaned over the bar, caught Barney by the shoulder, and talked fast in his ear. Cy leaned in close to listen. Betty whispered something that made Barney shake his head, then the three of them turned to look at Evelyn.

Evelyn smiled. Cy and Barney looked away; Betty stared back without smiling. Evelyn dug a candy kiss out of a plastic pumpkin on the bar, unwrapped it, and ate it. Betty was still staring at her. Evelyn rolled the wrapper from her candy into a ball and tossed it back in the pumpkin.

Betty's mouth fell open. She grabbed Barney, leaned over the bar, and nodded at the pumpkin. Cy put his hands on Betty's shoulders, turned her away from the bar, and kissed her on the shoulder; she tried to shake him off, but he held her tight, whispering in her ear.

Barney took the bar rag from his belt and wiped his way down the bar past Evelyn, moving the pumpkin onto the back bar as he passed like it was in his way.

Alice's head had come to rest on the neck of her beer bottle, and the drunk Evelyn had never seen before was grinning at her over Alice's back. He was fat-faced and bald. His scalp was red and his eyes were glassy; alcohol had dried to a shine on his chin and darkened like grease on the front of his plaid jacket. He pointed his glass at Evelyn and said, "You're so beautiful they all had to stop talking and look at you."

Barney turned around, slapped his hand down in front of the drunk, and yelled, "I told you not to be bothering people you don't know!"

Alice's head snapped up and she yelled, "I wasn't sleeping, god-damnit," before her head sank down over the bottle again.

Evelyn turned her back on them.

On the other side of her, Rudi was telling the guy in the blue suit that living in a small town didn't mean you had to become a small person. His back was like a wall blocking out the end of the bar, where she could hear Ozzie Minor and Norb Dombrowski laughing with a farmer.

She craned her neck, but all she could see was Norb sitting at the bar in a diaper. She tapped Rudi on the shoulder. Barney reached across the bar, caught her by the wrist and said, "I wouldn't do that."

Evelyn said, "Why? He don't bite."

"He's almost got that guy sold on buying Bill Ganyo's old house." Barney let go of her wrist and wiped his hand on the rag in his belt.

"I wish he'd move his fat butt so I could see who the hell I'm drinking with." Evelyn drained her glass and slid it forward for a refill.

Barney looked at the empty glass, then up at Evelyn and said, "Does Frank know you're here?"

"He'll figure it out when he gets home from work and I'm not there."

Barney picked up the glass, took it down to the tap and filled it.

Betty made a grab for Barney's arm as he turned away from the tap; then she saw Evelyn watching her and let her arm drop. Cy smiled at Evelyn over Betty's shoulder. Betty turned around and said something that made him stop smiling.

Barney said, "Twenty-five cents."

Evelyn slid him a quarter.

Alice DeGroot snored once and jerked her head up off her bottle. She was wearing a witch's hat, tied with black ribbon under her chin. The bottle had left a red circle in the middle of her forehead.

Evelyn said, "Happy Halloween, Alice."

Alice looked at Evelyn and said, "Oh, Jesus Christ."

"Don't bother Alice, now," Barney said. "She's having a nap."

Alice slid her bottle across the bar and stood up.

Barney said, "Where do you think you're going?"

"Home," Alice said.

"Sit down. We haven't had the costume judging yet."

"Remember what I'm wearing and compare it to everyone else's."

Alice backed away from her stool, looked Evelyn up and down, then lurched out the door. She didn't even look back when Barney yelled that he wanted to buy her a drink.

Cy said something under his breath, and Betty said, "Well, what'd you expect?"

Evelyn said, "That's the first time I've ever seen Alice walk out of a bar while she could still walk."

Barney picked up Alice's bottle, slammed it under the counter, went down to the end of the bar and leaned on it, talking to Cy and Betty.

Evelyn took a gulp of her beer. It made her choke and she had to put the glass down until she finished coughing.

When she looked up, the drunk in the plaid jacket was grinning at her again. His highball glass hung crooked in his hand; alcohol dribbled into his lap. He toasted Evelyn with the dripping glass and said, "I'm drunk."

"I know," Evelyn said. She pulled a Kleenex out of her dress pocket, held it to her mouth and turned to face the bar.

The drunk said, "I'm just trying to talk."

Evelyn coughed quietly into the tissue until the choking fit passed.

The drunk said, "What you come in here for, you don't want to talk to people?"

"I came in here to get drunk," Evelyn said. "Is that all right with you?"

The drunk leaned towards her, bracing himself on the empty stool. "Ladies don't get drunk in bars. Only assholes like me do."

Evelyn grabbed her glass, threw her head back, and gulped the rest of her beer. She shoved the glass across the bar for a refill and said, "Satisfied?"

"You sure don't drink like a lady," the drunk said.

"I'm not a lady. Now leave me alone."

"Please forgive me for talking to you." The drunk turned back to the bar, his shoulders slumped forward.

A curse and a stumble and Ozzie Minor was behind her, swaying, a Santa beard hanging from the left half of his face and a red cap on his head.

Evelyn said, "Looks like you got an early start, Ozzie."

"She was gonna win," Ozzie said.

Norb hollered from the end of the bar, "Ozzie, get back here before you fall on your ass."

"She was," Ozzie said.

Evelyn said, "What're you talking about?"

"Alice! She worked all week on that witch's hat and she was gonna win!"

Ozzie's eyes fluttered shut and he staggered forward. Evelyn put a hand out to steady him, but he jerked away yelling, "Keep your hands off me!" and crashed into the tables by the jukebox. Vera grabbed her champagne glass from the table and clutched it to her chest.

Barney shouted, "Ozzie, go sit down!"

"I'll go sit down somewhere people ain't afraid to drink!" Ozzie staggered to the entrance, ran into the bottom half-door, grabbed it to steady himself, and turned back to the bar.

Norb called out, "Ozzie, I'm drinking your beer."

Ozzie pointed a wobbly finger at Evelyn. "It's your fault," he said, then pushed his way outside and stumbled down the street.

The bar was quiet. Betty played with the prongs of her pitchfork and watched Barney. Barney was leaning against the beer cooler, arms folded, glaring at Evelyn.

Evelyn said, "What? Him and Alice get drunk and that's *my* fault?"

Barney said, "He ain't any drunker than usual."

The drunk in the plaid coat said, "He's an asshole."

"I told you to shut up," Barney hollered.

The drunk dropped his head between his shoulders like he was going to get hit.

Barney slapped his hand on the bar, pointed to a washtub set on two chairs between the bathroom doors and said, "Somebody go bob for them goddamn apples. I didn't haul that shit over here for my health."

Vera yelled from her table that Betty should do it.

Betty said, "I didn't spend two hours on my hair to go stick it in a bucket of water."

"Why not?" Barney said. "You're the one wanted a Halloween party."

Norb yelled, "Let Vera do it. She's dressed for it."

Vera said, "I tried already, but my crown fell in."

Everybody laughed. Betty smiled over her beer and let Cy put his arms around her.

Evelyn said, "Let's get Rudi to do it."

Betty raised her head from her drink. Her smile was gone.

Barney said, "Rudi don't want to bob for apples."

"I want him to," Evelyn said.

She reached across the empty stool to where Rudi was telling the guy in the blue suit that sending your kids to Catholic school only got them mixed up with the poorer classes. She said, "Come on, Rudi, let's see you get your suit wet," and tried to pinch him in the neck.

Rudi spun around swinging, knocking Evelyn's hand hard against the bar.

Barney yelled, "Hey!"

"Then do something about her!" Rudi shouted and turned back to the guy in the blue suit.

When Evelyn's hand hit the bar, it knocked over her beer glass. Barney caught the glass before it rolled off the bar and threw the rag from his belt into the puddle of beer.

Evelyn's fingers stung. She stuck her hand in her mouth and mumbled, "I guess when you're a big fat crook you don't have to get into the spirit of things."

"People got their own ways of celebrating," Barney said. "It ain't your place to be telling 'em how." He wiped the beer off the counter onto the floor.

Evelyn shoved a quarter across the bar. Barney looked at it.

"Well, *he's* not going to pay for my refill so I guess I'll have to."

"Christ," Barney said. He picked up Evelyn's glass, checked it for cracks, and took it to the tap, turning his back to Betty when she banged her glass down.

The jukebox kicked in with a song about Lisa. Evelyn drank off half her beer as soon as Barney slid it to her and turned toward the dance floor. Smokey was leaning on the jukebox, running his finger down the song list.

Vera stood up, straightening her crown, and tried to pull Jerry out of his chair. "It's Halloween. I wanna dance."

Jerry turned his back to her and growled, "Sit down."

Vera swung away from the table with her hands behind her head, her legs popping out of her swimsuit like ham hocks.

The drunk whispered to Evelyn, "They ought to put her on a diet before they let her out in a suit like that."

Evelyn said, "She's *been* on a diet."

The drunk whistled and spit flew out of his mouth. "Keep dancing, honey. You might lose some more weight!"

Vera dropped her arms and stopped dancing. She went back to the table and lit a cigarette.

Jerry said, "Are you happy now?"

Vera threw her match in the ashtray and fell into a chair with her back to the bar. The crepe paper was sagging; a black streamer floated down to the middle of the dance floor and hung there, swaying in the breeze from the door.

Evelyn stuck her glass out for a refill, but Barney just looked at it as he went past with a bucket of ice on his shoulder. He dumped the ice under the counter near Betty.

The drunk said, "I don't think he wants you to drink anymore. He didn't want to give me any more, but I made him."

Evelyn said, "He shouldn't have given you any more. You're drunk." She rapped her glass on the end of the bar.

Barney looked over his shoulder and said something under his breath.

Betty said, "Then why don't you?"

Evelyn rapped her glass harder.

Barney yelled, "I heard you the first time." He grabbed Evelyn's glass out of her hand and took it to the tap.

When he brought it back, Evelyn slid a quarter across the bar and whispered, "That man is bothering me." She nodded at the drunk.

Barney said, "He's bothering everybody." He rang up the quarter and went back down the bar to where Cy was fighting with Betty.

Betty was trying to get off her stool but Cy had her blocked in the corner, trying to hold her by the shoulders. She hit him in the chest with her fists, but he grabbed one of her wrists. Betty said, "Ouch! Damn it, that hurts." Cy let her go. Betty hopped off her stool and slipped under Cy's arm. Barney leaned over the bar whispering, but Betty yelled back, "Spirit of the season, my foot. This place is a goddamn funeral home!"

She threw her cigarettes and lighter in her purse. Smokey was playing with her pitchfork. She grabbed the pitchfork out of Smokey's hand, pointed it at Cy and said, "We're leaving now."

Barney said, "Now, Betty—"

She wheeled on him, pointing the pitchfork, and yelled, "I mean it."

Cy looked over at Evelyn, picked his bottle off the bar, nodded to Barney and said, "I'll take care of this." He walked past Betty, around the corner of the bar and towards Evelyn.

Betty said, "No!" and made a grab for his arm. She missed and came back to the bar, threw herself down on her stool, and slammed her purse on the counter.

Cy was a big man, wide-shouldered, with hands and arms like a giant's, and the black hat of his Lone Ranger costume made him even taller. He bent over Evelyn with his arms stretched out, saying, 'Here's my girl" and hugged her like a crane picking up dirt.

Betty leaned over the bar like she was going to jump on it.

Evelyn said, "You'd better be careful. I'd hate to die with your girlfriend's claws in my back."

Cy turned red. He said, "Betty's claws ain't that sharp," took a sip of his beer and stared at the floor.

Betty stood up and called Cy's name. Barney grabbed her by the arm and pulled her back down. Smokey slid down next to her, talking, putting a hand on her other arm. Cy put a foot on the rung of Evelyn's stool and said, "How're you doing?"

Evelyn said, "A few more of these and I'll be just fine." She drained her beer, held her glass out for Barney to see. Barney turned his back on her.

Cy said, "I mean otherwise."

"There is no otherwise," Evelyn said and rapped her glass on the edge of the bar.

Barney glanced over his shoulder then turned back to Betty. Evelyn banged her glass down hard; it sounded like a shot. The farmer at the far end of the bar said, "Jesus H!" Evelyn raised her glass to bang it again, but Cy caught her by the wrist and said, "You're drinking those awful fast, Evie."

Evelyn jabbed a finger into his chest. "I seen you so drunk you had to have Barney start your car."

Cy's mouth opened, but nothing came out. Evelyn snatched her glass off the bar and slid off her stool, shoving Cy in the chest. "Get the hell out of my way."

Evelyn's legs felt like rubber when her feet hit the floor. Her cigarette fell from her mouth. A stool came up to meet her; she grabbed at it and held on. Her glass hit the floor and the drunk's sweaty face blotted out the room.

The drunk said, "I don't care if nobody likes you—you're still beautiful."

"Who gives a shit?" Evelyn said and launched herself away from the stool, headed for the corner where Betty, Barney, and Smokey were cowering.

Then Cy's big hands were on her shoulders, holding her up, guiding her towards the jukebox. It was so easy to walk that she had to go along. Then she was in a chair, sitting at one of the tables by the dance floor, and Cy was kneeling in front of her with his hands on her arms, saying, "Can I get you something?"

"You can get me a goddamn beer," Evelyn said.

Cy studied her face, his jaw tight, then stood up, squeezed her shoulder and went back to the bar.

Evelyn reached for her purse but it wasn't on the table; it lay on the floor by the bar. Her cigarettes were scattered under the stools. She waved her hand at them like she didn't care anymore and turned to stare out the door.

Across the street, Chuck Williams ran past the theater with three bigger boys behind him. All of them were waving cartons of cigarettes over their heads. They turned left at the corner and headed towards the Red Owl, their laughter dying beyond the buildings.

Cy said, "What's so interesting out there?"

"Life," Evelyn said. She reached up for the glass of beer Cy held out to her. The glass was only half full. She said, "Are we on rations now?"

"Barney's changing the keg."

Evelyn drained the glass, slid it back to Cy and said, "Thank you."

Cy turned a chair around and straddled it. Evelyn turned away and stared out the window.

"I'm surprised you ain't home giving out candy, as much as you like Halloween."

"I like Christmas, too. That don't mean I'm gonna stay home for it."

She turned back from the window. "I never was one for staying home at night, Cy. You know that."

Cy looked her in the eye. She didn't look away. Finally he said, "We all heard about your being sick, Evie."

"Do I look sick to you?"

"You look just fine, Evie."

Cy turned red around the ears. He shot a quick glance back at the bar and cleared his throat.

Evelyn slid her chair back. "You ain't my doctor, Cy. You got no idea what's going on inside of me."

When she stood up the bar began to spin. She put her hands on the table to slow things down.

"Why don't you let me take you home?"

"I'm a big girl, Cy. If I wanted to be home, I would be."

Evelyn stepped around the table, brushing Cy off when he reached for her wrist. An orange streamer came undone and floated to the floor in front of her. When she stepped around it the room turned green. She fought her way through it and back to the bar.

Rudi was looking down at her as she pulled herself onto her stool. She muttered, "What the hell are you staring at?"

"The floor show," Rudi said and turned his back to her.

Evelyn's purse and cigarettes were sitting neatly on the counter now. She looked around for her glass, but it was still on the table where Cy was sitting. She called out to Barney. He ignored her, so she picked up an ashtray and banged it down on the bar.

Barney turned and yelled, "What?"

Evelyn said, "I want a drink!"

He came towards her scowling. "Where's your glass?"

"I lost it."

Barney grabbed a clean glass, went to the tap and filled it three-quarters full.

"Fill it up. I'm paying for it."

Barney gave the tap another pull. The glass overflowed. He set it down hard on the counter in front of her and said, "Make it last this time. You ain't in a race."

"Like hell I ain't."

Barney backed away from the bar, pulling on the rag in his belt. When Norb shouted, "Who do you have to kill to get a beer around here?" he moved quickly to the end of the bar to serve him.

Cy picked up the glass Evelyn had left behind and brought it back to the bar. When he tried to slip in between Betty and Smokey, Betty yelled, "Don't touch me!"

Barney yelled, "Knock it off, you two!" from where he was talking to Norb.

Cy leaned into Betty, trying to whisper in her ear, but she shoved him away, shouting, "Keep your filthy hands off me!"

Cy stretched out his arms. Betty slid back on her stool and pressed herself against the wall, screaming for Barney. Barney was lunging over the counter before Cy's hand reached Betty's shoulder. He put one hand in front of Betty, pointed the other at Cy and said, "Over in the corner. Now!"

Cy leaned against the doorjamb and muttered something at Betty over his beer.

"Then go take a goddamn shower!" Betty yelled.

Barney shushed her. Smokey slid closer and put his hand on

her shoulder.

The drunk nudged Evelyn and said, "That one's crazy."

"She's a tramp, too," Evelyn said.

The drunk leaned into Evelyn, laughing with his mouth open.

Barney slapped his hand down on the counter between them. "I told you not to be bothering people."

The drunk straightened up and hung his head.

Evelyn said, "He wasn't bothering me."

"He was bothering *me*," Barney said.

Evelyn pushed her glass across the counter and said, "Go fill this."

There was a scream from the end of the bar. Cy had come up behind Betty and put his hand on her bare shoulder. Betty whirled off her stool, pushing Cy backward. "You son of a bitch!" she shrieked, grabbing her neck where he'd touched her.

Barney bounded to the end of the counter, shouting, "Cy, get over by the window!"

Cy said, "Screw it. I'm leaving."

"You asked for this Halloween party—" Barney yelled.

Cy pointed at Betty and yelled back, "*She* asked for the Halloween party."

Betty yelled, "I didn't ask you to touch people full of disease!"

There was a gasp from Vera's table.

Cy glanced at Evelyn before turning to Betty. He said, "You want disease?" and moved towards her with his hands out. Betty screamed and tried to pull Smokey in front of her. Smokey broke away and ran to the other side of the jukebox.

"I'll give you disease!" Cy yelled. He grabbed Betty off her stool, rubbed his free hand across her face and down her neck, shouting over her screams, "How's this for disease?" He shoved his hand down the front of her dress.

Barney pulled a two by four as long as his arm from under the bar and slammed it flat on the counter. "That's enough!"

The room shook and fell quiet. The jukebox skipped once and went on.

Cy said, "Now *you* can go take a shower" and walked out of the bar, kicking the bottom door open with his foot. Barney put the two by four back under the bar.

Evelyn coughed. Betty's head snapped up and she stormed around the corner towards Evelyn.

"This ought to be good," Rudi said.

Betty stopped halfway to Evelyn's stool and yelled, "Why aren't you home where you belong?" Evelyn swung around to answer her but Betty went on, "Why didn't you just stay there and die?" She looked down at her arms, her hands, then at Evelyn who was gagging on a cough, and screamed, "I hope you go to hell!"

Betty ran back to the corner of the bar, grabbed her purse, and ran out the door.

Nobody moved and nobody talked. The bottom door swung back and forth.

Barney said, "The next one leaves before closing don't come back for a week." He grabbed Cy's bottle off the bar and glared at Evelyn.

Evelyn said, "Why don't you stick those eyeballs up your ass?"

The drunk guffawed. Smokey giggled and ducked behind his drink.

Rudi signaled for a refill. When Barney brought it, Rudi leaned across the bar and jerked his head in Evelyn's direction. "How much you figure that one cost you so far?"

"I ain't figuring."

"There's no reason you should lose your best customers for the sake of one drunk."

Evelyn yelled, "If we didn't have to listen to you selling death-traps to suckers maybe we wouldn't have to *get* drunk!"

Jerry laughed. Rudi turned around slowly and looked down at Evelyn.

"I know you," Evelyn said.

Rudi turned back to the bar, fished his wallet from his breast pocket, slid a dollar across the counter to Barney, and said, "Could I please have change for the jukebox?" He took his change and went over to the jukebox, making a wide circle around Evelyn.

The guy Rudi had been talking to had freckles, and hair the color of a carrot. He smiled at Evelyn and turned to stir his drink.

"What's so goddamn funny?" Evelyn said.

Barney said, "Give it a rest, Evie."

Evelyn said, "I don't have to take insults from someone dumb enough to buy a house from Rudi Erickson."

The guy turned back to her, his mouth tight, and said, "I wouldn't waste an insult on someone who's too drunk to walk."

"At least I ain't walking around in one of Rudi's rat traps," Evelyn said.

Barney wiped down the bar between them and said, "Be nice, Evie. It's a holiday."

Evelyn shoved her empty glass across the bar and said, "I told you to fill this." She swung around on her stool, turning her back on Barney before he could answer.

All the streamers on the ceiling had come undone by now and floated like the ghosts of trees over the dance floor. Rudi was bent over the jukebox, his fingers drumming the buttons.

"Play that Nat King Cole song about Lisa," Evelyn yelled.

Rudi said, "Play it yourself. You ain't dead yet."

Smokey's hand went to his mouth. Vera turned her face to the wall. Rudi pressed some buttons and the jukebox began playing a song with violins.

Evelyn turned back to the bar. She grabbed a cigarette from her pack, but dropped it on the counter when a cough ripped her throat. When she uncovered her mouth there was blood on her hands. She put them under the counter and wiped them on the skirt of her dress.

Rudi came back from the jukebox. The drunk watched him cut a semicircle around Evelyn and said, "Anybody walks around in a suit is an asshole."

Evelyn said, "What the hell are *you* wearing?"

"A blazer," the drunk said. "I'm wearing a goddamn blazer."

Barney rapped the counter in front of the drunk and said, "No swearing."

Evelyn said, "He ain't swearing. He's talking to me."

Barney went past without looking at her.

Rudi signaled Barney with his finger, leaned across the bar and said, "You know, you could solve your problem with a call to the mill."

Barney said, "Frank's got enough troubles right now. I ain't adding to 'em."

"What about your troubles?"

"I'm handling 'em." Barney wiped his way down the bar away from Rudi.

Behind Evelyn, Rudi said, "Aside from what *he's* losing, it's not fair to the rest of us."

Evelyn fumbled for her cigarette. When she looked up, the drunk was staring at her. Sweat oozed from his forehead. He clutched the bar with both hands, worked up a grin and said, "I like you."

"Thank you," Evelyn said.

"You're the only person in this whole goddamn bar I like." The drunk slid off his stool and said, "I'm gonna to sit next to you."

He pushed his drink ahead of him, guiding himself along the bar with one hand. Evelyn tried to signal Barney but he had his back to her, talking to Smokey. The drunk hauled himself onto the next stool, blew gin in her face, and said, "Now I can see how beautiful you are."

Behind them Vera clapped her hands and called out, "Party games! Party games!" Evelyn turned away from the drunk.

Norb was over by the washtub, tugging on his diaper as he looked over the floating apples. Suddenly he thrust his head down into the tub and came up, face dripping, gripping an apple by the stem between his teeth. Vera cheered. Jerry and the farmer clapped. Norb bowed towards Vera. The stem broke and the apple fell to the floor.

"Foul apple!" yelled the farmer.

Vera jumped up from the table yelling, "My turn! I wanna get wet!"

She sidled up to the bucket and studied the apples, while sliding the straps of her swimsuit down from her shoulders.

The farmer whistled.

Jerry yelled, "Pull your goddamn swimsuit up!"

"No, pull it down!" Norb hollered.

The farmer clapped his hands and shouted, "Down! Down!"

"Up! Up!" Evelyn cried, but Smokey's whistles from the end of the bar drowned her out.

Vera took a deep breath and pushed her head into the tub. When she came up her hair clung to her face but an apple was stuck in her mouth. There were cheers from both ends of the bar. Vera bowed in all directions.

"Sit down. You're making a fool of yourself!" Jerry said.

Norb shouted, "She is not. She's the most beautiful woman in the bar!"

"She's the *only* woman in the bar, you drunken ass," Jerry said.

Norb said, "It still counts!"

The farmer laughed. Vera took the apple out of her mouth, snuck a glance at Evelyn, and slunk back to her table.

Evelyn turned back to the bar. The drunk had passed out and was snoring, his face on the counter. She dipped her fingers in his glass and flicked alcohol in his face. The drunk sat up, blinking. Smokey flagged down Barney and whispered in his ear, holding him by the sleeve and nodding at the drunk's glass.

The drunk said, "What the hell was that for?"

"If you have to sit next to me, stay awake," Evelyn said.

"I don't have to sit next to you."

"Then move."

Barney came down the bar, glaring at Evelyn, and grabbed the drunk's drink out of his hand.

"Hey, I paid for that."

"The ice is melted," Barney said and dumped the drink under the bar. He fetched a clean glass from the back counter and poured the drunk another drink.

"I ain't paying for a fresh drink."

"Nobody's asking you to," Barney said, and turned to Evelyn. "Behave yourself, damn it."

"Bite my ass."

Barney leaned across the counter. "Don't make me throw you out of here, Evie."

"You and what army?" Evelyn flicked her ashes in the direction of the ashtray and turned her back on the bar.

Vera was back bobbing for apples. Her hair was plastered to her face and her suit was wet. Norb and the farmer were the only ones watching her. Norb clapped every time she came up with an apple and set it down next to the bucket.

"I think you just ran out of apples," the farmer said.

"Now I'm going to put them all back in." Vera bent over, grabbed an apple from the table in her teeth, and dropped it into the tub. Water splashed in her face. Norb and the farmer laughed. Jerry stood up, kicking his chair out behind him, and took his beer over to the jukebox.

Behind Evelyn, Rudi said, "It ain't helping him any, he gets off work and finds her too drunk to walk."

"Half the people in this bar are too drunk to walk," Barney said.

"There's a big difference between her and other people."

The *Beer Barrel Polka* kicked in. Vera started dancing with an apple in her mouth. Evelyn got dizzy watching her and had to turn and grab the bar before everything went black.

When the room came back to her, Rudi was saying, "—if you're too chicken, give me the phone and I'll call the guy myself."

Barney shook his head and went to serve Smokey.

The drunk leaned over, grazed Evelyn's cheek with a sticky hand and mumbled, "Hello, beautiful."

Evelyn slapped his hand away and said, "Knock it the hell off." She grabbed her glass and turned to face the dance floor.

Vera was in front of the jukebox bumping and grinding to the *Beer Barrel Polka.* Jerry pressed a few more buttons and headed back to the table without looking over at her. Vera jumped in front of him and shimmied, her hands over her head. The farmer whistled and Norb howled. Jerry walked around Vera without looking up but she danced up behind him and bumped her hip against his ass. He spun around and made a grab for her, knocking a chair out of the way. She ran out to the middle of the dance floor and they stood there glaring at each other. Norb and the farmer stopped laughing. Jerry went back to the table, and sat down. Vera started dancing again. When the music ended Rudi was saying, "—lost fifteen pounds but she still looks like a hog with that apple in her mouth."

Vera stopped dancing. Smokey giggled. Barney told him to shut up.

Vera took the apple from her mouth and let her hands fall to her sides. Jerry came up behind her, led her back to the table, sat her down, and put her fur coat around her shoulders. Vera pulled the collar tight around her neck. The jukebox kicked in again, playing the song with violins.

The drunk let out a loud sob, blowing snot out of his nose and bubbles into his gin. He looked up at Evelyn with a face full of tears.

Evelyn said, "What the hell are you crying about?"

"All my times in De Pere, I never met anyone like you."

"Well, ain't you lucky."

"I come through to sell—" The drunk broke down, dropping his drink on the carpet and covering his face with his hands.

Barney cursed. He came around the counter, picked up the drunk's glass, and took it back behind the bar.

The drunk took his hands from his face. It was splotchy and covered with snot. "Everywhere I go, people wish I wasn't there."

"You make me sick," Evelyn said.

"You're the only lady in a bar ever even talked to me."

The drunk climbed off his stool and fell against her, covering her with his oniony sweat. Evelyn tipped her head back, but he slipped an arm around her shoulder and mumbled, "That's why you're beautiful."

"Get your hands off me!" Evelyn yelled.

"I'm saying you're beautiful—" He stumbled closer. She pushed him away and screamed. Barney arrived and twisted the drunk's wrist, shouting, "Let her go. Now!"

The drunk backed away.

Evelyn said, "Thank you, Barney."

Barney pointed at her and said, "Thank you, hell! You cause any more trouble tonight, I'll throw you out that door myself!"

"All I been doing is trying to have a good time!"

"You wanted a good time, you should've stayed at home."

"You got no business—"

"This *is* my business!" Barney yelled.

Evelyn yelled back, "And this is mine!" She picked up her beer glass and threw it at him. It smashed against the mirror and shattered over the back bar.

The farmer at the end of the bar said, "Hey."

Rudi muttered, "Jesus H—"

Barney said, "That's it. You're cut off." He started pulling clean glasses off the back counter, stacking them next to the sink under the bar.

Evelyn yelled, "You think I give a shit?"

Barney said, "I don't really care." He cleared a corner of the back bar and began to brush the shards of broken glass onto the floor.

Evelyn leaned across the counter and shouted, "You think you got the only bar in town?"

Barney ignored her.

"You think I can't go over to Brewer's, where they don't let men talk like assholes and fat women dance in swim suits?"

Barney turned to her and yelled, "Go to Brewer's! I wish to hell you would!"

Evelyn said, "I'm going," and grabbed her purse and cigarettes. She slid off her stool but when her feet hit the floor the room started to spin.

Vera and Jerry flew by, Vera twisting jewels off her crown and Jerry with a bottle of Pabst stuck in his mouth. The farmer spun past, wearing a plastic pumpkin on his head like a bonnet, with Rudi behind him, holding Barney by the shoulder and saying, "*got* to call him now." Then a chair whirled up in front of her; she caught it and fell down hard into it.

They were all looking at her. Jerry was at the bar next to Norb and the farmer. The farmer still had the pumpkin on his head. Smokey was coming towards her, his devil horns slipping down again.

Rudi nodded at the drunk, who was sleeping with his head on the bar. Barney slammed an ashtray against the counter next to the drunk's ear. The drunk jerked upright. Barney leaned over the bar, put a hand on his shoulder, and spoke quietly in his ear.

Outside in the street a skeleton screamed.

Staggering through the chairs, Smokey had almost reached her when Evelyn pushed herself to her feet and fought her way through a thicket of crepe to the jukebox.

The jukebox had orange lights around the outside, blue lights around the inside, and more orange lights inside the blue lights. Evelyn ran her finger down the glass trying to find the song about Lisa, but the lights all melted into a pumpkin that grinned at her. When she shook her head, the pumpkin went away, but Smokey was standing beside her, a bottle in his hand and his head against the wall.

Smokey said, "It's one-eighteen."

Evelyn ignored him.

Smokey said, "The song you keep asking for, *Mona Lisa*. It's one-eighteen."

"I know what number it is," Evelyn said.

She ran her finger down to the buttons, pressed the one, muttered "eighteen" to herself, and pressed the one again. The numbers ran together. She closed her eyes and counted her way over to the eight; when she opened her eyes again Smokey was watching her over the top of his beer.

"How do you think Frank's gonna feel when he gets off work and finds you passed out on the sidewalk?"

"At least he won't find me in a devil's costume that my mother made me, with horns sticking out of my chin."

Smokey felt his chin and pushed the horns back up on the top of his head.

"You sure are a hateful bitch," he said. He put his hands on the jukebox, leaned over and said, "I'm glad you're gonna die." He put his bottle to his mouth and went back to the bar, reaching up to straighten his horns.

Evelyn coughed. It tore through her stomach and caught in her throat. She pressed her elbows into her stomach until the burning passed.

At the bar Barney yelled at the drunk, "That's why I'm telling you!"

The drunk backed away from the bar, knocking his stool over. "You got no business letting her in here!" He brushed his coat like it was crawling with spiders, stopped, stared at his hands, then yelled at Barney, "I'll take you to court, you son of a bitch!" He stumbled backwards towards the door. "I'll take every damn one of you to court."

Evelyn pushed herself off the jukebox and into the drunk's path. He backed into her, spun around, and shrieked, "Keep away from me!"

Evelyn yelled, "They're lying!" and grabbed for his arm.

He swung at her, shouting, "Keep your hands off me, you filthy bitch!" Evelyn fell back against the jukebox. *Mona Lisa* skipped and started up again. The drunk ran out, leaving the half door flapping behind him, yelling, "All you filthy sons of bitches—" at people on the street.

Evelyn pushed herself off the jukebox and toward the door. She collided with the door frame in time to brace herself for another cough. Barney called her name. Evelyn sagged against the door and stared into the street.

"Gimme the phone, I'm calling the mill," Rudi said.

The song with the violins came on.

Across the street, her son David came around the corner, his sister trailing behind. Connie yelled for him to wait. David stopped in front of the movie house, pushed his mask up on his forehead and shouted, "Hurry up!" Behind him the door to the movie house opened and Dale Lynkowski came out with a farm boy.

Dale froze.

The farm boy yelled, "Run!" and the two of them darted for the corner.

Evelyn lurched onto the sidewalk, calling out, "You boys!"

Dale grabbed the farm boy by the arm and brought them both to a stop. David and Connie looked over at Evelyn. Connie waved until David pulled her hand down.

A group of kids with bags on their heads poured round the corner from the dime store. The smallest of them yelled, "Little Lee!" and pointed at the farm boy.

The farm boy pulled away from Dale, ran to the corner, and disappeared down the block.

Dale yelled, "Lee!" and took off after him.

The little kid followed them, yelling "Little Lee, come back!" The rest of the group ran after her, pushing past David and Connie and shouting, "Deena! Wait!" Connie wrapped her arms around her bag to protect it. David stared at Evelyn, not moving when the kids bumped into him, his mouth tight, his eyes hard and black.

Evelyn backed through the doorway into the bar again. Her legs hit a chair and she sat in it. The violin song ended. A crepe streamer blew against her face in the breeze. A cough tore her stomach, made her grab the sides of the chair, When she could breathe again, Barney was kneeling in front of her.

He said, "Can I get you a soda water?"

"You can get me a beer," Evelyn said.

"I can't do that, Evie."

Evelyn yelled, "Why not? Smokey's so drunk he's got horns sticking out of his chin, and you're still giving him beer!"

"We're all trying to be understanding here, Evie," Barney said. "You're not making it easy."

"What have you got to understand?"

Barney ran his hand through his hair. "Frank's on his way here for you," he said and went back to the bar.

Evelyn stood up; the bar swayed in front of her. She closed her eyes to keep it from tilting further but that made it worse, and when she opened them she wasn't facing the bar anymore. Vera was alone at a table, hunched over her drink, her fur coat covering her swimsuit.

Evelyn stumbled towards the table, fighting her way through streamers that caught at her face. She bumped against Vera's table and dropped into a chair, trapping Vera between the table and the wall. Vera called out, "Jerry?" but the *Beer Barrel Polka* drowned her out.

Evelyn said, "My kids can kiss my goddamn ass."

Vera said, "Jerry's sitting there. He's coming right back."

"My own kids, treating me like shit."

Evelyn coughed, spitting onto the table before she could cover her mouth. Vera pulled her hands onto her lap and flattened herself against the wall. Evelyn ran her arm over the wet marks her spit had made.

"I'd like to get out, please."

"Why? You lose a couple pounds, you ain't got time for my problems?"

"We've all got problems."

"Somebody called you a hog. You call that a problem?"

Vera pushed against the table but it wouldn't move. She sank down into her coat. "Please leave me alone."

Evelyn reached for her purse but it was still on the bar next to Rudi. She mumbled, "goddamn crook," turned to Vera and pressed two fingers flat against her lips.

"What?"

"A cigarette. I lost my purse."

Vera dug her cigarettes out of her pocket, shook two onto the table and shoved the pack back in her coat. Evelyn put a cigarette in her mouth, handed the other one to Vera.

"Keep it."

Evelyn dropped the cigarette on the table and sat staring at Vera with the other one hanging from her mouth.

"Christ," Vera muttered. She dug a book of matches out of her purse and tossed them across the table.

Evelyn had trouble getting the book open, then tearing out a match. When she tried to strike the match she missed and the match flew out of her hand. She held the book out to Vera.

"If you're too drunk to light a cigarette, you're too drunk to smoke!"

Evelyn dropped the matchbook and the cigarette fell out of her mouth. She put her fists over her eyes and burst into sobs that she fought to hold in her throat.

"Stop it," Vera said.

"He didn't want to know me. My own kid." She flattened her palms over her face and sobbed until tears ran down her arms.

Vera lit a cigarette and waved her hand for Barney, but he wasn't looking.

"I never even wanted any goddamn kids."

Vera stared at her cigarette, let Evelyn cry herself out.

After a while, Evelyn wiped her nose on her arm and said, "Did you want all those kids you had?"

"I had 'em, didn't I?"

"But did you want to? If you'd known how it was going to turn out?"

"It ain't over yet," Vera said.

Evelyn leaned forward, her hands grabbing the sides of the table. "What if it was? What if you woke up coughing tomorrow, and they told you you were sick? Would you be glad you had those kids?"

"I ain't sick," Vera said and stood up, pushing the table into Evelyn's stomach.

"If you coughed up some blood and they said you were dying, would you feel like it was enough?"

"At least I'd stay home and die like I was supposed to!"

Evelyn stood up, gripping the table. Vera yelled for Jerry.

Barney yelled, "Evelyn, goddamnit!" Jerry came tearing across the room.

"You wouldn't stay home and die like they told you," Evelyn said. "You'd know that wasn't enough!" She reached for Vera's arm.

Vera screamed, "Don't touch me!" and shoved the table, tipping it over on Evelyn.

Evelyn fell backward and her head hit a chair, then the floor. The table rolled off her.

Stools scraped and feet shuffled.

Smokey yelled, "Don't anyone touch her! There's blood!"

When Evelyn opened her eyes a circle of faces was looking down at her. Jerry had his arm around Vera. Barney was pushing through between Rudi and the man with red hair. Norb was backing away, shaking his head, but Smokey was bending down, staring in her face.

The farmer said, "Call an ambulance."

Barney said, "Frank's coming."

Rudi said, "Just throw a sheet over her. They're going to have to do it sooner or later."

"That isn't funny," Vera said.

Evelyn raised herself on her elbows. All the faces blurred together then separated again. Her forehead felt wet and there was a brown spot in her left eye. Smokey scurried away.

Barney said, "Lay down."

"Go to hell," Evelyn said.

"You fell down, so stay down."

"I didn't fall down. I got pushed."

Vera started to cry.

Smokey said, "We should put a pillow under her head."

"I ain't got no goddamn pillow," Barney said.

The door creaked open and everybody looked up. There were footsteps near her head, then Frank was bending over her in his oily work clothes. "Jesus," he said.

The others backed away.

Frank slid his hand under her head and said, "You okay, Evie?"

"Get away from me," Evelyn said. She heaved herself to her knees, grabbed the back of a chair and pulled herself into it. The room went green. When she could see it again, Frank had his arm around her.

Frank said, "You need to go to the hospital, Evie."

"I don't need a hospital," Evelyn said. "I need a drink."

"No."

"Don't you friggin' tell me what to do."

Evelyn pushed herself away from Frank's arm and out of the chair. Her hands were sticky and the brown spot covered her left eye. She could only see half of the bar. She headed towards the back, where Jerry, Norm, and Vera were gathered, but a chair sprang up and caught her in the stomach. She had to grab it and hold on. She waved her arm at the bar and yelled, "Don't *any* of you friggin' tell me what to do!"

From the part of the bar she couldn't see, Barney said, "Frank's your husband, Evie. Maybe you ought to listen to him."

Evelyn yelled, "All I want is a drink!"

Jerry leaned over the bar and whispered into the darkness. Barney's head came out of the darkness, nodding. Jerry put his arm around Vera and they walked into the brown spot and towards the door. Evelyn yelled after them, "Is there anything wrong with wanting a goddamn drink?"

Norb pulled his coat on over his diaper and stared at the floor. Barney looked at Rudi. Rudi set his drink down, folded his hands on the counter and said, "I think we'd all be a lot happier if you'd leave."

Frank put his hand on her shoulder.

Evelyn yelled, "*You'd* be happier! "What about me?"

Norb looked up and said, "You're sick, Evelyn."

The rest of them nodded.

Evelyn shook her fist at them and shouted, "There's nothing wrong with me! God *damn* you cocksuckers! I'll show you there's nothing wrong with me!"

She turned for the door, knocked over a chair, and slammed into the jukebox, then the wall. Frank came towards her. She threw a chair in front of him, shoved herself through the swinging door, and staggered into the street.

There was traffic but she stepped out in front of it. A car full of skeletons slammed on its brakes and a car from the other direction swerved around her. Something with a mop on its head yelled, "Bitch!" out of the rear window. She yelled back, stumbled back up the curb, and braced herself against a street sign.

Frank came out of the bar. Rudi was on the step behind him. She pushed off from the street sign and headed down Broadway towards Brewer's Tap.

She bumped into the building on the corner face first, but the brown spot in her eye diminished to a blur. She turned the corner by the dime store, and almost ran into the little farm boy walking along with Dale Lynkowski. The kid shrieked and ran around her. She yelled "Farmer!" at him; the kid shrieked again and ran faster, Dale close behind him. Frank came across George Street carrying her coat.

She lurched on towards Brewer's. The Budweiser sign in the window was lit and she could hear laughter inside, but she couldn't get the door to open. She backed up to give it a kick and saw she was in front of the door to the shoe shop. She pushed open the door to the bar and the laughter stopped.

Vera was at the bar. She put her hand on Jerry's shoulder and stepped behind his stool. Betty was leaning against the pinball machine talking to Cy. She was wearing a Japanese kimono and had a towel around her hair. Cy's face was red and his hair was wet. Betty saw Evelyn and said something under her breath. Eddie the bartender came to the end of the bar with a towel in his hand and said, "Evelyn." Alice DeGroot looked up from her bottle and said, "Oh, Jesus Christ."

3
CHUTES AND LADDERS

When Dale wouldn't stop chasing him, Little Lee dropped his candy bag, doubled back, and ran into the dime store. Fat Man Durant came charging from behind the register, shouting, "Out! Get out! You've been in here twice already!" Little Lee ran under his arm, down an aisle piled high with yarn divided by color and needles divided by size, past witches' hats piled up on the floor, and out the store's back door into the alley.

Dale was waiting for him, sitting on the back of a car with a candy cigarette in his mouth.

"Where do you think you're going?"

"He was chasing me, Fat Man Durant." Little Lee sat on a garbage can to catch his breath.

"Liar. You were running home to your ma."

"I wasn't running. He was chasing me."

"Well, he ain't chasing you now."

Dale threw Little Lee's candy bag at him. Little Lee stood up like he was going to catch it but took off running instead.

Dale jumped off the car, head down, and butted Little Lee in the shoulder. Lee fell on his back in the gravel and dirt.

"You think I'm gonna let you rat to your ma and have people at school calling me snitch?"

"If it was *your* brother, you'd tell."

"If it was *my* brother, he wouldn't be a farmer."

"You don't even know what a farmer is."

"I know they like to lay in the dirt."

Little Lee stood up, wiping his hands on his candy bag. He said, "I wanna go back to our neighborhood."

"We came downtown and we're staying downtown. It's bad enough I'm stuck with a farmer. I ain't hanging out with a rat who runs home to his ma."

Gravel crunched at the end of the alley. Dale ducked into the dark of the dime store's back doorway, pulling Little Lee with him. The crunching got louder. It sounded like people walking on snow.

A girl's voice said, "I'm telling Ma."

David's sister Connie hunched her shoulders and came down the alley, her brother close behind her kicking gravel at her back.

"Go ahead," David said. "By the time you check all the bars there won't be any gravel left to kick."

He aimed straight at Connie's head. A piece flew off to the side and hit Little Lee, making him catch his breath.

David looked up at the doorway. Dale stopped breathing.

Connie said, "She can't go in a bar, she's—"

"Let's go," David said.

"Where?" Connie said, but he was already pulling her out of the alley.

Little Lee said, "He saw us."

"Shut it," Dale said.

Little Lee tried to slip past him, but Dale grabbed him by the arm, saying, "This way, asshole." They turned down the alley, heading away from the theater.

Somebody nearby yelled "Farmers!" and Little Lee ducked back into the doorway. The kids in the paper-bag masks ran past the mouth of the alley, the tall kid in back. A rock hit the tall kid's shoulder; another flew past him and struck a girl at the front of the group. The tall kid scooped up the girl and they all disappeared down the block.

Four hoboes ran after them, one Lee's size, one taller, the other two only about three feet high. They stopped at the end of the alley. The tall kid threw a rock the size of his fist, yelling. "Run back to your goddamn farm!"

Dale put his hands to his mouth and hollered, "Lininger!"

The tall kid looked down the alley, his hands over his eyes. He said, "You picking garbage, Lynkowski?" and came towards Dale, the other hoboes behind him.

"That's your Dad's job," Dale said.

Lininger had a square head, big ears, and a silver front tooth. The kid Lee's size had a red crew cut and was chewing on a corncob pipe. The younger kids had charcoal beards. Lininger jerked his thumb at the doorway and said, "Who's the fat kid?"

The kid with the crew cut shouted, "He's a farmer!" and scooped up a handful of gravel. Lee pressed his face into the corner of the doorway.

"He ain't a farmer," Dale said.

Lininger said, "Diablo says he is."

Dale said, "He lives next door to me."

"He's Lee Van Vonderan. He's in my class," Diablo said and threw his gravel. It scattered across the doorway and Little Lee squealed in the dark.

Lininger turned around, kicked gravel at Diablo, and yelled, "Knock it off!"

"What are you now? The farmer's friend?" Diablo said.

The little kids laughed.

"Anybody throws rocks around here, it's gonna be me," Lininger said.

Diablo raised his foot to kick gravel at Lininger, spun around and kicked it at the little kids instead.

Lininger turned to the door and said, "Fat kid, come out here."

Little Lee stepped out of the doorway, his shoulders hunched forward, his eyes on the ground.

Lininger walked around him, looking him up and down.

Dale said, "You guys been to the priest's house yet?"

Lininger said, "They're giving holy cards. Who wants 'em?"

"We're going down Broadway. You guys can come with us if you want," Dale said.

Lininger stopped in front of Little Lee and sniffed the air. He turned to Dale and said, "We'll go with you, but this farmer ain't coming along."

Little Lee said, "I'm not a farmer. I live on Ontario Street."

"Ooooh! Ooooh! He lives on Ontario Street! Fancy schmancy!" Lininger waved his wrists like a girl. Diablo and the little guys laughed.

"At least he don't live over a store," Dale said.

Diablo and the boys stopped laughing.

Lininger glared at Dale, then at Lee, turned back to Dale and said, "Ditch him."

Dale said, "I can't. I promised I'd watch him."

Diablo said, "Promised who? Frances the Talking Mule?"

Dale took a step towards Diablo, yelling, "I promised my ma!"

Lininger hooted, "You promised your ma?" He nodded in the

direction of the street. The other boys staggered out of the alley, laughing.

Dale hollered, "Wait—"

Lininger spat in the gravel by Dale's feet, then wiped his mouth with the back of his hand. "You want somebody to wait for you? Go ask your ma." He stalked out of the alley and turned the corner by the theater.

Dale grabbed Little Lee by the wrist, dragged him down the alley. When Little Lee asked where they were going, Dale said, "Down Broadway," and yanked his arm so hard he fell to his hands and knees on the gravel.

Dale screamed at him to get up.

"It wasn't my fault," Little Lee said, pushing himself to his feet.

"It *is* your fault!" Dale yelled. "It's all your fault. People won't talk to me 'cause I'm stuck with a farmer!"

Lee yelled back, "Those guys wouldn't talk to you 'cause you're a baby afraid of your ma!"

Dale ran at him. Little Lee scrambled towards the dime store hollering, "Leave me alone!"

A voice at the end of the alley said, "There they are."

Dale spun around and Little Lee came out of the doorway; they both started backing away. Chuck was coming down the alley towards them with the three big guys from the drugstore behind him. The guy with the pimples said, "You even think of running, we'll kick your asses clear over to Wrightstown."

They stopped in front of Dale, smiles on their faces. Little Lee ducked behind Dale. Chuck leaned over Dale's shoulder and said, "You run home to your ma yet?"

Dale said, "He ain't going anywhere."

"Nobody's asking you," Chuck said.

Dale said, "Go to hell."

The pimply guy pointed his finger at Dale and said, "You. Out of the way."

Dale looked over his shoulder at Lee hunched over behind him.

The pimply guy took a step forward and Dale moved out of the way.

Lee stood up straight.

The blond guy with the crew cut said, "Do it, squirt."

Chuck moved in on Little Lee, grinning like a demon. Little Lee turned to run but Chuck grabbed him by the collar and said, "Give me your candy, farmer."

"No," Little Lee said. His hands started to shake, rattling the candy in his bag like popcorn.

The dark-haired guy said, "Take it. We're gonna be late."

Chuck grabbed the bag, but Little Lee wrapped his arms around it, pulled it to his chest, and screamed for Dale.

The big guys turned on Dale. Dale backed away. The guy with the pimples said, "Ain't you gonna help your friend?"

"Why? It's not my candy," Dale said.

The pimply guy laughed, turned back to Chuck and said, "Come on, asshole. You gonna let a farmer whip your ass?"

Chuck slammed his fist into Little Lee's stomach through the candy bag. The bag exploded and candy flew out. Little Lee fell to his knees gasping for breath. Chuck held the bag in the air. A sucker fell out and hit Little Lee on the head.

The blond yelled, "Way to go, squirt!"

The dark-haired guy said, "Now let's get the hell out of here."

Their footsteps crunched out of the alley before Lee could breathe again. When he looked up, only the pimply guy was left. He was holding Dale by the hair, saying, "—go anywhere near his mom and the same thing'll happen to you." He shoved Dale

away from him, strolled to the end of the alley, and headed down
George Street past the theater.

Dale got to his feet, tucked his candy bag under his arm, and
picked at his hand where a stone had broken the skin. Little Lee
knelt in the gravel, his costume torn at the elbow; he pinched the
two pieces together and let out a sob before he could stop himself.

Dale said, "They wouldn't have hit you if you hadn't acted like a
baby."

"They didn't hit me because I was a baby," Little Lee said. "They
hit me because they wanted my candy." He pushed himself to his
feet and stomped off towards George Street.

Dale yelled, "You think those guys ain't watching you?"

"I don't care," Little Lee yelled back.

"You think they won't kick the shit out of you before you get to
your ma?"

Little Lee stopped walking. He stuck his head around the corner of the theater onto George Street and quickly pulled it back.

"They said they might hurt your ma if you told her."

Little Lee leaned against the wall of the theater; his belly shook
and tears poured down his face.

Dale turned his back on Little Lee, dug a Bit-O-Honey out of
his bag, ate it. When Lee stopped crying, Dale said, "You can get
another candy bag from Durant's. We'll hit the stores again, and
you'll get all your candy back."

Little Lee said, "I can't go back in Durant's. He chased me out
last time—"

Dale said, "'Cause you went running in like a scaredy-cat."

Little Lee sniffed and eyed the back door of the dime store.

"We'll get so much candy, those guys'll wish they left you alone."
Dale clapped his hand on Little Lee's shoulder and shoved him

through Durant's back door.

Mr. Durant was handing a gumball to a girl in flower costume when Dale and Lee came up the aisle from the back of the store. When he saw them, his smile faded. "I thought I chased you out of here."

Dale said, "We came for a bag."

"I don't sell bags."

"We want a candy bag. He lost his." He pushed Little Lee towards the register.

Mr. Durant looked at Lee and said, "They're five cents apiece."

"They're supposed to be free," Dale said.

"You want a free bag, buy something."

Dale muttered, "Fat—" under his breath and dug in his candy bag for change. He dumped three pennies on the counter. "That's all we got."

Mr. Durant scooped up the pennies and slid a small bag across the counter.

Dale said, "We wanted a big one."

"And I wanted five cents," Mr. Durant said.

Little Lee snatched the bag off the counter and ran out the front door.

"See if we come in your stinking store again," Dale said.

Out on the sidewalk Dale cupped his hands to his mouth, and yelled, "Fat Man Durant's got ants in his pants!" He grabbed Lee by the collar and they took off around the corner onto George Street, stopping outside the movie theater to catch their breath.

Dale said, "You should have made him give you a big bag."

"He's a grown-up," Little Lee said. "You can't make grown-ups do things."

They were still breathing hard when they went inside the theater. Mrs. Vincent leaned over the candy counter and said, "My goodness, is there a ghost after you?"

Dale said, "We're in a hurry. The stores are closing."

Mrs. Vincent dug in her apron pocket and dropped a penny in each bag.

Dale said, "Last year we got popcorn."

"Maybe last year you weren't in such a hurry," Mrs. Vincent said.

Outside, Little Lee said, "She'd have given us popcorn if we waited."

Dale reached in Lee's bag, dug the penny out, and said, "You still owe me two." Then he shoved Lee down the block towards Broadway.

At the library, Dale got a Dum-Dum and Lee got a Milky Way. When Dale handed his Dum-Dum back and asked for a Milky Way, the librarian said beggars couldn't be choosers, snatched the Dum-Dum out of his hand, and put her face back in her book. Out on the sidewalk, Dale took Lee's Milky Way and said Lee still owed him a penny.

They got oatmeal cookies at the root-beer stand. Dale threw his cookie back at the vendor, yelling, "I don't eat garbage," and it hit her in the head. She chased them for half a block; they ran for three.

When they stopped, Dale said, "You should have thrown yours when she was chasing us. She might've slipped on it."

"I like oatmeal cookies," Little Lee said and headed down the block.

There were two gas stations at the end of Broadway. The Sinclair station had round green pumps and a greasy old man who hobbled out to pump your gas. The old man's shack was full of men playing cards; they each gave Lee and Dale a nickel from their winnings, and the old man unlocked the candy machine and gave them each a Hershey bar.

The Citgo station had tall bright lights, silver pumps, and a guy in a glass booth who gave them each a gumball. Dale whispered, "Tell him the guy across the street gave us candy bars," but Lee walked off across the parking lot.

Dale caught up to him and said, "Wait till I tell the kids at school somebody gave you a gumball and you were too chicken to do anything about it."

"He gave *you* a gumball and you ain't doing anything about it," Little Lee said.

"I don't have to. Everybody knows I ain't a chicken."

Little Lee walked away. Dale jumped in front of him, flapping his elbows, making chicken sounds. Little Lee yelled at him to stop.

"They'll call you the chicken farmer!" Dale said and clucked circles around Little Lee until he dug the gumball out of his bag and went back to the booth.

The guy looked up from a magazine with a girl in a devil costume on the cover.

Lee held up the gumball.

The guy said, "You want me to fill that up for you?"

Little Lee said, "No," but nothing came out of his mouth.

"You want me to eat it?" the guy said.

Lee looked at Dale kicking the curb on the far side of the parking lot, turned back to the man in the booth and said, "My friend said to tell you the gas station across the street is giving out candy bars, not stupid pieces of gum like this."

The guy yelled, "What?"

"He wants something better," Little Lee said.

The guy came out of the booth, rolling the magazine into a tube. Little Lee ran for the sidewalk. The magazine hit him in the back of the head and he dropped the gumball. The guy yelled, "And don't come back, you fat little shit!"

Dale grabbed Lee off the sidewalk and pulled him behind a tree.

Dale said, "You gotta play a trick on him."

Little Lee said, "I think he's calling the cops."

"He can't call the cops just 'cause you asked for something."

"We can go back to the library. I'll go through the line twice and get you a Milky Way."

"You want the kids at school to know you let somebody get away without giving you something?"

"He gave me a gumball."

"You gotta call him something."

"Huh?"

The guy was in the parking lot, picking up his magazine.

Dale said, "Call him a farmer."

"No," Little Lee said.

A bunch of fourth-graders ran down the other side of the street, headed for the Sinclair station.

Dale cupped his hands over his mouth. Lee grabbed his arm and said, "Don't—"

"Yell it," Dale said.

Lee stepped out from behind the tree, his bag clutched tight to his chest, and yelled, "Hey, farmer!"

The guy in the booth turned a page of his magazine.

Dale said, "Louder."

Little Lee yelled it, louder.

The guy stuck his head out of the booth, hollered, "Say what?"

Dale stepped out and yelled, "He said you're a farmer with shit on your shoes!"

He gave Lee a shove and they took off towards town without looking back.

It was almost closing time, and Broadway was packed with kids fighting to get in doorways, bumping into each other on the sidewalk, running after each other across the street. Lininger's hoboes chased the paper-bag kids out of the dry cleaners as Chuck and his friends came out of Greasy Joe's diner chasing girls. Chuck tripped Lininger as he ran past. Lininger fell to the pavement, rolled over, and came up ready to punch, but Chuck was already a block away, yelling "Garbage picker!" over his shoulder. Lininger ran after the paper-bag kids, who had just disappeared down the alley behind the diner.

Dale and Little Lee got M&M's at Greasy Joe's, pennies from the dry cleaners, and popcorn balls from a furniture shop.

Little Lee stopped in front of Brewer's Tap to shake his bag and make more room in it. Dale grabbed the candy and dumped it into his own bag, saying he'd give Little Lee his when they got home.

Little Lee said, "How are you gonna know—"

Then someone screamed "Lynkowski!" and Lininger's gang came running at them through traffic. They jumped the curb and crowded Dale and Lee tight against the bar's window.

Lininger punched Little Lee in the shoulder and said, "Lose your candy bag, farmer?"

Diablo said, "I hear Chuck Williams looked at you and you dropped your bag and ran."

Dale said, "Chuck Williams wouldn't talk to you if you had the same ma."

"He didn't have to," Diablo said. "He talked to Tim Lindquist and I got it from him."

"You believe a patsy that can't even walk?"

"At least he ain't a mamma's boy who hangs out with farmers."

"At least I ain't a rat whose dad sells junk he stole from the dump!"

Diablo lunged at Dale, but Lininger tripped him. Diablo hit the sidewalk and jumped up, his fists raised at Lininger. Lininger snorted, "Don't even think about it."

Diablo swung his shoulders to straighten his jacket, spat on the ground, and cursed.

Lininger poked Little Lee and said, "Where's all your candy if Williams didn't take it?"

Diablo said, "He probably ate it."

"He threw it out in the road so Chuck couldn't get it," Dale said.

"Shit," Diablo said.

Dale jabbed Little Lee in the back and said, "Didn't you?"

Little Lee nodded. When the two little kids laughed, he said, "I did!"

"Then how come we didn't see any candy laying around?" Lininger said.

Little Lee said, "A bunch of cars ran over it."

"And then those farmers with the paper bags picked up what was left," Dale said.

"That's just like a farmer," Diablo said, "picking dirty candy off the street."

"At least Chuck Williams didn't get it," Dale said.

Lininger said, "What did Williams do when you threw your candy in the road?"

"Nothing," Little Lee said.

Diablo laughed.

"I threw a rock at him and he ran away."

"You fat, lying farmer, you didn't pick up any rock!" Diablo said.

"I ain't a farmer! I hit Chuck Williams with a rock!"

Lininger said, "Then how come he wasn't hurt?"

Lee looked down at the bag in his hands. "I hit him in the back.

When he saw me pick up the rock, he turned and ran."

Diablo said, "What about the other guys?"

"When they saw Lee grab a rock they started running, too," Dale said.

Diablo yelled, "Bullshit—"

"I ain't seen you take on any of them sixth-grade assholes, Diablo," Lininger said.

The little boys laughed.

Diablo said, "That farmer didn't take on no sixth-graders."

"I saw him do it," Dale said.

Diablo pointed at Little Lee and sputtered to Lininger, "Make him prove it!"

Lee said, "I can't prove it. They ran away."

"Then you can fight somebody else," Diablo said.

"No," Little Lee said and backed up against the wall.

"Come on. You can prove how brave you are. You can fight me."

"I don't want to fight you."

"'Cause you're a coward."

Dale said, "He ain't a coward."

"Why's he hanging onto the wall, then?"

"He don't like to fight," Dale said. "He's afraid he'll hurt somebody."

Even Lininger laughed.

"He'd've smashed Chuck's head with that rock if I hadn't stopped him."

Diablo said, "I ain't afraid of no rock."

"Let 'em fight," Lininger said. "If Diablo gets killed we'll leave him at the convent to scare the nuns."

"That farmer's gonna be the one scaring the nuns," Diablo said.

Lininger stepped away from Diablo and Dale stepped away from Lee. The smaller boys moved closer, trapping Little Lee with

Diablo against the wall of the bar. Diablo put his fists up. Little
Lee twisted the front of his costume into a knot and screamed,
"Leave me alone!"

"Fight him!" Dale said. "Show him you're not afraid of him!"

One of the little kids said, "Come on, Diablo! Kick his ass!"

Lininger crossed his arms and said, "Is that how you kept
Williams from taking your candy?"

Dale yelled, "Show him, Lee!"

"Yeah, farmer," one of the little kids shouted. "Show him how
you wet your pants!"

Little Lee pulled his hands out of his costume and yelled, "I'm
not a farmer!"

Diablo yelled, "You look like a farmer to me—a chicken farmer!"

Little Lee spun around, fists up, shouting, "Stop calling me
that!"

A girl's voice yelled, "Little Lee!" and Diablo jumped back.

The kids in the paper-bag masks came pouring around the corner. The littlest of them caught sight of Little Lee and ran forward.
The others saw Lininger and stopped, calling for the little girl to
come back. The tallest of them took off his mask and worked his
way to the front of the group.

The little girl put her arms around Little Lee's waist and said
through her mask, "We seen you before."

Diablo said, "Now tell us you ain't a farmer."

"I don't know her," Little Lee said and shoved the girl away.

The girl fell to the sidewalk laughing, and pulled the paper bag
off her head. "It's me, Deena!" she said, and turned to the kids behind her, "Lee didn't even know who I was!"

The tall kid picked her up. "Come on, Deena," he said, and
carried her back to the group. One of the other kids picked up her
mask and candy.

"Come on, Lee," the girl said. "We're going to your house for cocoa."

The bag-heads turned to look at Little Lee.

"Lee isn't coming with us," the tall kid said.

The girl said, "Why not?"

"Because we don't want him to."

The bag-heads turned away from Lee and walked in a group to the corner.

Inside the bar people were singing, *All I want for Christmas . . .* A man yelled, "Evelyn puked behind the slot machine!" A woman screamed.

Little Lee watched the kids standing at the corner. When the light changed and they stepped into the street, he cupped his hands and hollered, "Farmers! Stupid fat farmers!"

One of the kids looked back; the tall kid pushed him ahead without stopping.

Lee ran to the corner and shrieked, "You got shit on your shoes! All of yous!"

The kids crossed the street and turned the corner without looking back.

Lee shrieked, "All of yous!" again and his voice cracked.

A fat man wearing a diaper walked past Lee and went into Brewer's Tap.

When Lee turned around, Diablo had his fists up and his head cocked, and was rolling his shoulders.

"You're still gotta fight me, asshole."

"I don't gotta fight anybody."

Dale said, "He fought the farmers. Leave him alone."

"He didn't fight 'em," Diablo said. "He just called 'em names."

"He only called them names because they had better costumes than him," Lininger said.

Little Lee yelled, "You go to hell!"

Lininger said, "What'd you say to me?"

"He didn't mean it," Dale said.

"My mom bought this costume in a store!"

Lininger slapped Diablo on the back and said, "Kick the shit out of him."

Diablo jumped forward and poked Little Lee in the face. Little Lee turned his face to the wall and screamed, "Get away from me!"

Somebody giggled.

David came running around the corner holding a Slo Poke over his head. Connie came chasing after him. When they saw Dale they stopped short.

Diablo grabbed Lee by the ear and said, "Here, tough guy. Maybe you can beat up the cancer kids."

"Shhh!" Dale said and stepped behind Lininger.

Connie said, "Don't even talk to him." She took David by the arm and turned him back to the corner.

"What's your hurry?" Diablo said. "We got a farmer here wants to fight with you."

David slowed. Connie whispered fiercely to him and they kept walking.

Diablo twisted Lee's ear and said, "Tell 'em you want to fight 'em, farmer."

"No," Little Lee said. He slumped to his knees.

Diablo yanked him back up. "Why not? You beat up Chuck Williams, you should be able to beat these rejects."

Little Lee said, "I don't fight people with cancer."

Lininger laughed.

David pulled his arm away from Connie and turned to face them.

"You made him mad now, farmer. You better apologize," Diablo said, shoving Little Lee towards David.

Little Lee said, "I don't apologize to people with cancer."

"You shut up about cancer!" David yelled.

Dale told Little Lee to be quiet. Lininger winked at him.

Little Lee said, "How can I shut up about cancer when I don't even *talk* to people with can—"

David was on top of him, dragging him to the ground. Little Lee covered his head and fell face down, screaming for Dale to help him. David's fists slammed into his head. He could hear guys yelling, "Kill the farmer!" and Connie bawling David's name. He caught sight of Dale behind a lamppost, then David brought both fists down on the back of his head. There was a crack; his mask snapped and fell to the sidewalk.

Little Lee got to his knees, shrugging David off him. David came at him again, his fists raised, spit on his breath. Lee put his head down and charged. David hit the sidewalk still swinging his arms. Lee pummeled David's head with the palms of his hands. Lininger hollered, "Use your fists, you asshole!" Little Lee clenched his fists, but David grabbed at him, and when he jumped up, the front of his costume tore off in David's hands.

David scrambled to his feet. Lee looked down at his dirty T-shirt through the gaping hole in his costume and began to cry.

"Now you can be a pig farmer, you fat-bellied freak!" David said.

Little Lee screamed, "You cancer-faced creep! I'll kill you!" and swung at David, catching him on the side of the head and knocking him to the ground.

"Holy shit!" Diablo hollered.

When David hit the sidewalk, Little Lee jumped on his chest and started beating him around the head. Connie was screaming for her mother. Diablo kept shouting, "Holy shit! Holy shit!"

Lininger hollered, "Kill the son of a bitch!" Even Dale was yelling, "Hit him, Lee!"

A drunken voice hollered, "What's going on out here?" Everyone stopped yelling and backed away. The drunk called out, "Evelyn! Jesus Christ!" A crowd came out of the bar, a red light flashed, a siren blared, and a giant hand pulled Little Lee off David and held him dangling in the air. Little Lee's T-shirt caught under his arms. He tried to wriggle out of it, but the guy who had hold of him yelled, "Knock it off, buster!" The guy had wet hair and smelled of baby powder.

A cop car stopped in the middle of the street, its light flashing. Lininger and Diablo were a block away, the smaller hoboes running after them. Dale darted around the cop car and ran straight into the cop. David lay on the sidewalk, his knees pulled up to his chest. Two guys in party hats stood over him, beers in hand. A woman in a swimsuit filled the doorway of the bar, more faces behind her.

"You're breaking my arms," Lee yelled.

The guy who had hold of him pushed him down against the wall and told him to stay there. The cop tapped Dale's shoulder and pointed over at Little Lee. Dale went over and stood next to Little Lee, his back to the wall.

David pulled himself up against a lamppost.

The cop came to the curb and said, "Who started it?"

Little Lee pointed at David.

David said, "The farmer did."

"I ain't a farmer! I live here!" Little Lee shouted.

The cop came up on the sidewalk. "If you live here, how come I've never seen you before?"

"Maybe you weren't looking."

Dale jabbed Little Lee in the shoulder.

The cop said, "I think we'd better find whoever brought you to town and get you sent home."

"You should send him to jail," David said.

The cop laughed and put a hand on David's shoulder. "I can't send somebody to jail for being a farmer."

"You should put *him* in jail so he can't touch anybody!" Little Lee yelled. "His mother's got cancer!"

The cop took his hand off David's shoulder.

"Shut up!" David screamed. His voice cracked and he started to cry. Connie tried to touch his arm, but David shoved her away.

"You're Evelyn Schmidt's boy?" the cop asked.

The woman in the swimsuit got pushed out of the doorway and Evelyn tottered out of the bar. Her dress was torn and her face was smeared with blood. She crossed the sidewalk on unbending legs and grabbed hold of the lamppost where David stood crying.

"What the hell have you got to cry about?" she said. She tried to grab him, but lost her balance and had to clutch the lamppost again to pull herself upright.

Then she saw the cop and said, "Good evening, Walt."

The cop said, "You alone tonight, Evelyn?"

"You're the goddamn cop."

A couple of people laughed. David glared at them.

The cop turned to Connie. "Is your father home, honey?"

Evelyn said, "How the hell would she know?"

Connie backed away from her mother.

David said, "Mom—"

"Well, does she look like *she's* at home?" Evelyn said.

David pushed himself away from the lamppost. Evelyn reached for his arm. She missed and fell to her hands and knees.

The cop moved towards her, his hands outstretched. A woman in a kimono said, "Don't—" The cop dropped his hands and nodded to David. "Help your mother up."

David put his hand under Evelyn's arm, but she shoved him away and used the lamppost to pull herself up until her face was level with the cop's. She cleared her throat and spat on the sidewalk in front of him. The cop jumped back.

"You son of a bitch," Evelyn said.

An old black car squealed around the corner and came to a stop next to the cop car. Frank Schmidt climbed out. Connie ran to him and he picked her up. The cop walked over and started talking quietly to him.

"Stop talking about me!" Evelyn yelled. She stepped off the curb and stumbled. David caught her and she held onto his shoulder.

The cop turned to Evelyn and said, "We were talking about your son."

"There's nothing wrong with my son."

"He's been picking fights with other boys."

Evelyn looked across at Dale and Little Lee. "I saw those little bastards before. They were picking fights, not him."

Little Lee yelled, "We didn't go near him!"

"You're a lying little farmer!" Evelyn shouted.

David yanked himself away from her and yelled at her to shut up. She staggered forward and made a grab for him. Frank set Connie down and caught Evelyn before she fell. The cop put a hand on David's shoulder.

"I saw them," she said.

David yelled, "You didn't see anything!"

"I saw them run away from you."

"You didn't see anybody! You're too drunk to see anything!"

Evelyn pulled away from Frank and slapped David's face.

David caught his breath and looked hard at his mother. "I hate you!" he screamed.

Evelyn's mouth fell open.

David pulled away from the cop and pounded his fists against his mother's stomach. "I hate you and I hope you die!" He turned and ran across the street, past the drugstore and around the corner.

Evelyn's hands went to her stomach.

The cop yelled for everyone to go back inside. A woman's voice crackled over the car radio and the cop ran to answer it.

Evelyn coughed and gagged; dark spit dripped down her chin. Frank touched her arm, but she shrugged him away and staggered off in the direction David had gone, her legs stiff.

The cop came back to the curb and said, "I got a call, some kids setting fires over by the fairgrounds—"

"They're on their way home," Frank said, nodding across the street.

The cop rubbed his hand across the back of his neck and said, "We heard about Evelyn. We just— It's a damn shame, you know?"

"Thanks, Walt."

The cop stood and watched as Frank put Connie in the car and drove off.

A guy in a diaper said, "That boy'll be sorry he ever talked to her like that."

The crowd shuffled back into the bar, and the street was empty except for Little Lee and Dale and the cop.

The cop squatted down in front of Little Lee. In the bar behind them, the jukebox started up.

"Do you know what cancer is?" the cop said.

Little Lee nodded.

"Then you know better than to fight with people who have it."

"I didn't want to—"

"You got any scratches?"

The cop took Lee's hands, looked at both sides of them. Lee began to shake. The cop said, "You'll be okay." He squeezed Lee's shoulder and went back to his car.

Little Lee ran to the curb and yelled, "Am I gonna get cancer?"

"I think you were lucky this time," the cop said. He got in his car and drove off.

Lee turned his hands over and pulled at a fingernail with a red spot on it. His hands shook, but when he clasped them together to hold them still his shoulders shook and he couldn't see anything. Then his head shook and it looked like his hands were full of spots that wouldn't stop moving.

A car full of screaming boys went past.

Dale jumped up laughing. He spun around, kicked the wall of the bar below the window, and yelled, "Wait till we find those cowards!"

Little Lee tore back the sleeve of his costume and ran his hand up and down his arm, whimpering.

"They ain't gonna be calling you a chicken farmer when they hear how you told off that cop!"

Little Lee tore back his other sleeve.

"Ain't nobody gonna mess with us anymore. They're gonna be lucky we even talk to 'em!" Dale grabbed Lee in a headlock.

Lee shook him off. "Leave me alone!"

"Nobody's ever gonna call you farmer again."

Little Lee screamed, "I don't care about farmers! I got cancer!"

Dale froze, his mouth hanging open. "You ain't got cancer."

"You don't know!"

"That cop said you didn't have cancer."

"Cops don't know about cancer. They know about arresting people. I could've got cancer from getting hit in the head and he wouldn't even know where to look."

Little Lee pulled his T-shirt up, picked at a red mark on his stomach, and started to sob.

"You're crazy," Dale said.

"You're the one who's crazy! Making people get cancer so you can show off to your friends!"

"At least I got friends. If it wasn't for me you wouldn't have any friends in this town."

"I don't need you for friends. I got friends you don't even know."

"Farmers!"

"Even a farmer's better than you."

Little Lee turned and headed for the corner. Dale caught up with him and blocked his path in front of the dime store.

"Where you think you're going?"

"Home."

"You ain't going home. I don't care if you *die* of cancer."

"I ain't listening to you anymore," Little Lee said and pushed past Dale. Dale grabbed him by what was left of his costume, and it came off in his hands.

Lee's eyes widened as if he was going to cry.

"God *damn* you!" he shouted and punched Dale in the nose.

Dale's head jerked back. His hand went to his face, and when he brought it down there was blood all over it.

"You son of a bitch!"

"You're the son of a bitch!" Lee shouted and hit him again.

Dale staggered backwards, both hands to his face. Lee rammed into him, head down, knocking him to the ground.

"I ain't afraid of you!" he screamed and beat Dale around the head with his fists.

Dale twisted under him, using his arms to try and deflect the blows. "Leave me alone!" he yelled.

"Why didn't you leave me alone when your friends were pick-ing on me?" Little Lee yelled back. "Why didn't you leave me alone when I wanted to go home?"

He pinned Dale's shoulders with his knees, lifted his fist and drove it down into Dale's face.

Dale screamed. He spat blood from a busted lip and began to bawl. Little Lee jumped up and stood over him. Dale rolled him-self into a ball.

"I hope *you* get cancer!" Little Lee yelled. "I hope your whole *family* gets cancer and dies!"

Then he turned and ran. Past the post office where Superman was trying to kiss Batgirl, past Ford's bakery where Mr. Ford was eating a Tootsie Roll behind the glass door, past the convent where Lininger was fighting with Diablo, past Superior Street, and Huron, and Erie, to Ontario, and down Ontario to the house in the middle of the block where his mother stood on the front porch, waving at his cousins who were piling out of their station wagon and running up the steps, holding up their candy bags, their paper-bag masks still on their heads.

4

BOYS IN THE DARK

It was cold in Legion Park, and black. The moon hung high behind the frozen clouds, gleaming dimly off the metal picnic grills beside the woods at the top of the hill, and casting a pale glow over the frosted grass of the ball field a few blocks away, but leaving the flat land of the playground in deepest gloom.

From his perch on top of a picnic table, Steve Omsted could barely pick out the white sleeves of the jackets on the boys below him—Spinelli on the bench, and Casey in the grass with a bottle of brandy on his chest. Somewhere in the night a girl screamed like a siren.

A few feet away, Steve's brother, who everybody else just called Omsted, said something that made his friends giggle. There were four of them sitting in the swings, black shapes barely outlined by the weak rays from the streetlight that hung on a wire over Ontario Street a block away. He knew Carner and Rusch; the other one was a little runt Steve hadn't seen before.

The wind rocked the streetlight, and the house on the corner cast a huge darting shadow across the tennis court like a dark hand trying to grab the night. The moon slipped out from between the windblown clouds and gave everything in the park the faintest blue halo.

Spinelli looked at his watch.

"He'll be here," Steve said.

Spinelli let his hand drop.

"You don't know shit about farmers. You think he's gonna pass up a date with Jeannie?"

"Christ, you're crabby," Casey said. He uncapped his flask and poured brandy down his throat.

"You get drunk and fuck this up, you'll find out what crabby is."

Spinelli said, "Nobody's gonna fuck anything up."

"What are you?" Steve said. "A goddamn fortune teller?"

Spinelli climbed off the picnic table, lit a cigarette, and blew smoke at a tree.

From over by the swing set Rusch said, "Hey, Steve. I hear when Haskins asked Jeannie to homecoming he tried to kiss her on the lips."

Casey giggled in the grass.

Steve climbed off the picnic table and stood over him.

"He was making a joke," Casey said.

"It won't be a joke when I stick that bottle up your ass."

"Christ, I was having more fun handing out candy for my old man."

Casey stood up, shoved his brandy in his back pocket, and stumbled towards the shack where the skaters warmed up in the winter. He pulled on the door but it wouldn't budge.

Rusch hollered for Casey to kick the door down.

"You little assholes keep your butts in them swings and shut up or you're outta the park," Steve growled.

Casey slammed his foot against the door of the shack.

Steve grabbed him by the shoulder. "God damn it! You're gonna draw the cops."

"It's Halloween," Casey said. "Even the De Pere cops got better things to worry about than somebody breaking into an empty shack." He zipped Steve's jacket up to his neck, then turned and jumped, caught the edge of the shack roof, and pulled himself up.

Steve grabbed at Casey's leg but missed. Casey stood up on the roof, laughing, Steve yelled that he was going to kick Casey's ass and slammed his shoulder against the wall of the shack, rocking it. Casey put his hands out, balancing like a tightrope walker. The kids on the swing set laughed. Spinelli told them to can it. Then he came up behind Steve and said, "He's right. There's kids waxing windows all over town; he ain't gonna draw no cops."

Steve spun around. "What are you now? A fucking expert on everything?" He jabbed his finger at Spinelli, and yelled, "You don't know shit!"

Spinelli breathed deeply and said, "Fine. I don't know shit." He went back to the tree by the picnic table and leaned against it, arms folded, staring at Steve over the glow of his cigarette.

Rusch said, "I guess we know who got Steve's spot on the team."

"Shut it, Rusch," Omsted said.

Steve turned to the swings. "Say what?"

Carner giggled. The other boys stared at the ground.

"Okay, Spuds," Steve said. "I want you and your little asshole friends out of the park."

Omsted said, "My name ain't Spuds."

Steve yelled, "I'll tell you what your goddamn name is," and charged the swing set. Carner screamed and ran, bumping into the runt and knocking him over. Steve grabbed the chains of his brother's swing and tried to shake him off, but the kid held on. Spinelli put his hand on Steve's shoulder. Steve shrugged him off, yelling, "Get your hands off me!"

Spinelli said, "Look" and pointed over at Ontario Street.

An old station wagon with no right fender clattered to a halt in front of Putzie's house. The back doors opened, and a dozen kids spilled out, all of them with paper bags on their heads. A skinny guy slipped out of the front on the driver's side; a fat woman hoisted herself out on the other, sending a creak of metal crawling up and down the street.

"It's a barrel load of monkeys," Spinelli said.

The light over Putzie's front door blinked on, and a wispy-haired woman came out, slipping a book into the pocket of her housedress. The kids pushed each other across the yard and onto the porch, crowding around her and shoving their open candy bags in her face. The fat woman waddled up the sidewalk, holding her purse open like a trick-or-treat bag, and squealed something that made the woman in the housedress laugh.

"Those are Putzie's cousins," the runt said.

Steve said, "No wonder they got bags on their heads."

"Too bad there ain't a bag big enough for the fat one," Spinelli said.

Steve threw his head back and laughed.

A fat kid in a tattered costume came running round the corner at the other end of the block, pumping his arms and screeching like a factory whistle. The woman in the housedress ran into the front yard and caught him as he ran across the lawn. The kid yammered and flailed his arms, then threw himself tight against her, pointing behind him at the lights of downtown.

The fat woman hauled herself back down the steps and put her hand on the sobbing kid's back. The skinny guy rubbed his knuckles on the kid's head and the three of them waited till he'd cried himself out. Then the woman in the housedress took him by the hand and all four of them started towards the house.

The fat kid froze when he saw the kids on the porch lined up like a wall of bags, watching him. The man tried to nudge him forward but he wouldn't move until the kids on the porch turned their backs on him and filed into the house. The fat woman followed them; she had to turn sideways to fit through the door. The skinny guy put both hands on the fat kid's shoulders and walked him into the house. The woman in the housedress went in last, stopping for a minute in the doorway to look towards downtown. Then she closed the door, the light blinked off, and the street was dark again.

Steve said, "That place even *looks* like a farm since they moved into it."

"It always looked like a farm," Spinelli said. "They just brought the smell."

"It did not," the runt said.

Spinelli said, "How would you know? You were probably born in a barn yourself."

"That used to be my house."

Steve turned and asked his brother, "Who is this little runt?"

"I'm Chuck Williams."

"Your old man oughtta have his ass kicked for selling to a bunch of farmers," Steve said.

"Why? We ain't living next to 'em."

Steve went up to the tree where Chuck was sitting. "So you ruined the place for their neighbors. You ever think of that?"

Rusch said, "He don't care. He just moved in and ruined *our* neighborhood."

Spinelli came up next to Steve and said, "That true? You one of them new families been stinking up our neighborhood?"

"We've already been there three months," Chuck said.

"That's about when the stink started," Spinelli said. "You're probably part farmer and don't know it."

Steve kicked Chuck's foot and said, "You part farmer, runt?"

"Leave him alone," Omsted said.

Steve walked over to the swings. "Say what?"

"He ain't a farmer." His brother stopped swinging by putting his feet down hard.

Steve said, "I'll decide who's a farmer around here" and lunged forward.

His brother jumped off the swing and ran past him, and when the swing came back down it clipped Steve on the side of the head. He put his hand up to check for blood. Rusch and Carner giggled in the dark.

Spinelli said, "You oughtta be ashamed of yourselves, hanging out with somebody who's half goddamn farmer. Next thing he'll be teaching you how to barn dance."

Steve yelled, "What the fuck do you know about barn dancing?"

"I was backing you up," Spinelli yelled back.

Steve charged Spinelli. "I've had enough of your fucking backing me up!"

"Fine. Handle it." Spinelli went back to the picnic table and sat on the bench. He kicked his legs out in front of him and shoved his hands in his jacket pockets.

Steve followed him, his fingers jabbing the air. "You get my spot on the team, all of a sudden you think you know everything?"

Spinelli looked down at his shoes. "I said handle it."

"You don't know shit," Steve said.

Spinelli looked up at Steve and smiled. "I must know something. I ain't the one who flunked off the team."

Carner giggled. Rusch backhanded him in the chest.

Steve pointed at Spinelli. "You get your ass kicked out on the field, you're gonna *wish* you flunked outta school."

"A guy with brains don't have to worry about people kicking his ass," Spinelli said.

"Any guy afraid to get his ass kicked belongs with the cheer-leaders, not on the team!"

Spinelli came off the bench, fists up.

There was a crash from the shack. Casey clung to the roof and slowly got to his feet again. Brandy bottle in hand, he began to sing the school fight song, with the words changed to point out that Spinelli's brains wouldn't do much good if they didn't stay in his head.

Steve slammed himself against the shack, and screamed, "Shut up!"

Casey broke off, laughed and pointed at Spinelli. "That guy just called you the biggest moron in De Pere."

"I don't care if I'm the biggest moron in the goddamn world! I don't need any shit from you!"

Carner and Chuck and Omsted laughed. Steve wheeled around, fingers jabbing the air, and screamed, "*Fuck you!*" He stormed back to the picnic table and threw himself on the bench next to Spinelli. Spinelli slid down to the other end.

The moon crept back behind the clouds, taking the silver glow from the edges of the night. The boys by the swing set disappeared into the darkness, where their whispers rustled along with the dead leaves.

Rusch hissed, "You gotta take one."

"No I don't," Chuck said.

Carner said, "Not smoking just proves you're a baby."

"I didn't say I didn't smoke. I said I didn't want one."

Rusch said, "We'll make you want one, asshole."

Spinelli slid down the bench towards Steve, the letter on his jacket the dimmest glow in the night. "You'll be off probation second quarter. Basketball won't even have started yet."

"What's the point in basketball?" Steve said. "You learn to play it, then in a few months you graduate and you never play it again."

The wind ripped through the park and pulled the clouds away from the moon. The moon hit the swing set with a sliver of light. Chuck was sitting under a tree, with Rusch and Carner standing over him.

Carner said, "What'd you do? Promise the nuns you'd give up smoking for Lent?"

"Lent's not till next year," Chuck said.

"You got plenty of time to quit, then," Rusch said. He bent down, flipped his pack open, and said, "Smoke up."

Chuck pushed the cigarettes away, went over to the swing set, and sat down next to Omsted.

Rusch said, "Omsted, tell your friend to get over here and take a cigarette."

"He doesn't want a cigarette," Omsted said.

Rusch said, "I don't trust anybody that doesn't smoke."

"You don't know anybody that doesn't smoke," Carner said, jumping out of the way when Rusch took a swing at him.

There was a ripping sound from the roof of the shack. Casey stood up with a long, jagged piece of wood in his hands, yelled, "Heads up, assholes," and hurled it at the picnic table. It stuck in the ground by Steve's feet like a spear.

Steve jumped up. "You fucking moron, you're gonna kill somebody!"

"Eventually," Casey said.

He pulled up a bigger piece and hurled it in the direction of the swing set. It landed just in front of Carner, who jumped back and shrieked. Rusch tossed his cigarette, pulled the spear out of the ground, and ran after Carner, whooping like a cowboy. Carner ran around the swing set, dodging between the poles, crying for help.

Steve yelled, "Both of you, knock it off!" He caught Rusch by the hood of his sweatshirt as he ran past, yanked the spear out of his hand and shoved him towards Carner.

He stuck the spear in the ground next to the one by the picnic table and turned to yell at Casey, but Casey hissed, "*Somebody's coming!*" and dropped flat on the roof of the shack.

Spinelli jumped off the picnic table, shoved his hands in his pockets, and pointed with his chin towards Ontario Street. A woman in a housedress, a scarf on her head and a sweater over her shoulders, was headed into the park.

Steve said, "Nobody move."

"It'll look like something's up if nobody's moving," Spinelli said.

Steve said, "Get rid of your cigarettes." He threw his cigarette down and ground it in the dirt.

The wind picked up, blowing away the clouds and flooding the park with moonlight. The woman stopped by the swing set. It was the woman who'd come out of Putzie's house when the station wagon pulled up. She held her sweater around her neck with one hand; the wind ruffled it like a cape behind her.

"Is one of you boys named Omsted?" the woman said.

Steve broke a cigarette in his pocket. Spinelli whistled part of the school fight song, stopped.

"Well?" The woman looked from the swings, then to the picnic table, then to the top of the shack.

Steve pointed over at his brother and said, "That guy's named Omsted."

Carner giggled. Spinelli muttered "Christ" under his breath.

The woman looked from Spinelli to Steve, then went over to Omsted. She stood in front of him until he stopped dragging his feet in the dirt and looked up.

The woman said, "Are you Omsted?"

"I might be," Omsted said.

"My son Leroy just came home and told me someone named Omsted was waiting to kill his brother Paul in Legion Park. Is that you?"

Steve whispered, "Shit."

The woman looked around at Steve, waited, then turned back to the swing and said, "Well?"

"I don't know anybody named Paul," Omsted said.

Chuck whispered, "Putzie."

"Shut up," Rusch muttered.

"I think you boys sometimes call him that," the woman said.

She stared at the boys on the swings but the boys didn't look back at her. Then she came around the swings to the picnic table and stood close to Steve, watching his face.

Steve said, "Ma'am?"

"Is your name Omsted?"

Steve slid a cigarette out of the pack in his pocket; it flipped out of his fingers and fell in the grass.

"No, ma'am."

The woman looked from Omsted back to Steve and said, "You're sure of that?"

"The only Omsted I know other than the one over there," Steve said, "is in Green Bay tonight at an ice-cream social."

Carner giggled.

The woman waited until he stopped, then said, "Paul and Leroy have had a hard time moving to the city this year, Paul especially. Now I know that town boys and boys from the country don't always get along—"

"I don't know your son, ma'am, but the Omsted I know's not the kind of guy who'd kill anybody."

"I grew up on a farm," the woman said. "I know how town boys can be."

She turned to look at them all: at Carner and Rusch under the tree, at Omsted and Chuck on the swings, at the roof where Casey was hiding, at Spinelli, then finally at Steve. Steve crushed a cigarette to dust in his pocket.

"I know how boys like to talk, and I know they don't always mean what they say. I'm sure if this Omsted knew how difficult it was for Paul to move into town he wouldn't say things he doesn't mean."

"I'm sure he wouldn't, ma'am," Steve said.

"And I'm sure if he realizes I know his name, and if Paul gets into any kind of fight tonight, any kind at all, I won't hesitate to call the police, he'll be more careful what he says in future."

"Yes, ma'am."

She looked around the group once more, then said, "Good night, boys," turned and walked out of the park, under the creaking light over Ontario Street and into the darkness.

As soon as she had disappeared, Steve lunged for the swings, knocked his brother to the ground, and jumped on him. Chuck hopped off his swing and ran away. Carner yelped and backed Rusch into a tree. Steve slapped his brother across the face, yelling, "You stupid little fuck! I told you to keep your mouth shut!" He brought his hand up and balled it into a fist. "I'll kill you, you little bastard!" His brother yelped. Spinelli's hand caught Steve's wrist an inch above his brother's head.

Steve let his arm go limp and stood up. Spinelli released his grasp. Omsted curled into a ball, whimpering.

Steve said, "Now take your friends and get the hell out of here."

"I'm telling Dad!"

"Go ahead! Tell him how you cried like a baby in front of your friends!"

His brother sat up. "I'm gonna tell him you got kicked off the team!"

Steve caught his brother by the jacket, yanked him upright, and brought his free hand back in a fist. Spinelli grabbed Steve's arm again. Omsted fell back to the ground, sniveling.

Steve yanked his arm out of Spinelli's grip, stood over his brother, and spat at him. His brother flinched.

"Candy-ass freak."

Steve turned, pushed his way past Spinelli, threw himself onto the picnic table, and lay staring up at the sky.

Spinelli came over to the table, lit a cigarette, and stared at Steve over the orange flame.

Steve said, "What?"

"You didn't tell him yet?" Spinelli said.

"What do you care?"

Casey sat up on the roof of the shack and said, "Your old man's gonna care when he gets to the game and you ain't even on the team."

"At least I won't be passed out under the bleachers with a bottle hanging out of my mouth."

Steve shoved himself off the table and leaned against a tree.

Omsted kneeled in the dirt, wiping Steve's spit off his sweat-shirt with a handful of leaves.

Chuck peeked out from behind a tree.

Omsted said, "What the hell are you looking at?"

"Nothing," Chuck said and backed away into the dark.

Omsted went over to the swing set and threw himself onto a swing.

Carner giggled.

Omsted kicked stones at him and Carner ducked.

Spinelli dropped one hand onto Steve's shoulder, and in the other held out a pack of Marlboros with the top flipped back. Steve shook his head.

"She won't let him out now anyhow," Spinelli said.

"He ain't home for her to let out," Steve said. "Or she wouldn't have been over here talking to us."

He turned to face Spinelli and said, "Christ, even an asshole like Haskins can think faster than that."

"Don't compare me to him! I ain't like that son of a bitch!" Spinelli headed back to the picnic table.

Steve followed him. "A stab in the back is a stab in the fucking back!"

Casey yelled, "Hey, assholes!"

A spear landed between them and stuck quivering in the ground.

Steve jumped.

Spinelli shouted, "You stupid drunk, you're gonna kill somebody!"

"You're killing each other anyhow!" Casey dug his bottle out of his pocket, held it out to Spinelli and said, "Why don't you have some? It might save your life."

"Go to hell," Spinelli said, and slouched against the table, his back to the park.

Casey sat on the edge of the roof, his legs dangling over the side.

He took a drink, waved the bottle at Steve, and said, "You know what you guys's problem is?"

"You," Steve said.

"You don't drink enough."

Steve turned his back on Casey. A gang of kids, their bags heavy with candy, trailed down Ontario Street, skirting the park.

Casey said, "I'm serious."

"You ain't ever been serious in your life," Spinelli said.

"What have you ever been serious about? Getting Steve's spot on the team?"

Steve snorted.

"I didn't ask for his spot on the team."

"But you got it anyway," Casey said.

Spinelli said, "Screw you."

Steve grinned up at Casey.

Casey waved his bottle at Steve and said, "And what have you been serious about? Jeannie Erickson? She's going to homecoming with some other guy and no matter how many farmers you kick the shit out of, it ain't gonna change that."

"Maybe I'll just kick the shit out of you," Steve said.

Casey pulled his legs up as Steve grabbed for them. "Go ahead. Kick the shit out of everybody. That ain't gonna change the fact that next year Jeannie'll be at college wearing Tim Haskins' pin and you'll be working at your old man's hotel, hoping to hell the bastard leaves it to you when he dies."

"Or I could be in jail for climbing up there and wringing your goddamn neck."

"That's what I'm saying! It don't matter what you want or what you do, 'cause something else is gonna happen anyhow. Stuff changes, and there ain't shit you can do to stop it."

Spinelli said, "And when are you gonna change?"

Casey thought a minute. "When they stop making booze, I guess."

Spinelli came over to the shack and looked up at Casey. "You're a real fucking moron. You know that?"

Casey said, "I might be, or I might not. The point is—" He took a long drink, raising the bottle to Spinelli as he swallowed, "I'm too fucking drunk to care." He flopped backward, laughing, and disappeared into the dark on the roof of the shack. Steve lay back down on the table.

Under the tree, Rusch held his cigarettes out to Chuck and said, "I ain't asking this time. Take one."

Chuck said, "I don't want one."

Rusch said, "People in hell don't want popsicles either."

"Yes, they do," Chuck said.

Rusch got him in a headlock, shoved the cigarettes in his face, and said, "Take one now or I'll ram the whole pack down your throat."

Chuck kicked Rusch in the ankle, ducked under his arm, and ran behind Omsted's swing. Rusch came after him. Chuck grabbed Omsted as a shield, but Omsted yelled, "Knock it off!" and shoved Chuck in the chest. Chuck fell backward in the dirt. Carner slipped up behind him, grabbed his arms, and pulled him off the ground. Rusch moved in, waving the cigarettes.

Chuck tried to twist out of Carner's grip.

Rusch said, "Omsted, tell your little asshole friend to take a cigarette."

Omsted turned around to look at Chuck, who stopped struggling.

"Take a friggin' cigarette," Omsted said.

Chuck said, "I don't want one."

"Then get the hell out of here," Omsted said and turned his

back on him.

Rusch shoved a cigarette in Chuck's mouth. Carner reached from behind and lit it. Chuck let the cigarette hang between his lips.

Rusch said, "Draw on it, asshole."

Chuck drew on the cigarette and coughed. The cigarette fell out of his mouth and landed in the dirt. Rusch picked it up.

Carner said, "I bet he gets sick."

"Tough." Rusch shoved the cigarette back in Chuck's mouth and said, "Drag on it like you mean it this time."

Chuck drew on the cigarette. His face flared up red, then he gagged and coughed at the same time. Carner jumped back. Rusch put his arm around Chuck's shoulder and said, "You're gonna smoke every puff of that, pal. I don't care if you puke your guts out."

The picnic table creaked. Steve looked up and saw Spinelli hunched over, elbows on his knees, staring at him.

A firecracker went off downtown.

Spinelli said, "You got no right blaming me for anything that's happening to you."

"Then how come you got my place on the team, my girlfriend ain't going to homecoming with me, and even farmers are saying hello to her in the hall?"

Spinelli jumped off the bench, yelling, "Tim Haskins taking Jeannie to homecoming has got nothing to do with me!"

"He wouldn't have asked her if I was still on the team."

"And you'd still be on the team if you hadn't flunked English!"

"He didn't ask her 'cause I flunked English. He asked her 'cause you got my place on the team!"

Spinelli ran his hand through his hair. "You're stupid, Steve, you know that? That's why every damn thing in the world is happening to you—because you're too fucking stupid to know when you're full of shit!" He headed for his bicycle.

"At least I ain't so stupid I gotta knife my friends in the back to get on the goddamn team."

Spinelli spun around. "I got a right to be on that team!"

"Because I ain't on it!"

"Because I'm better than you!" Spinelli screamed and charged.

Steve stepped into Spinelli's charge, fists up, but Casey landed between them. He put his hands out and shoved them both in the chest, knocking them into the grass.

Casey looked up at the roof of the shack like he wasn't sure he'd ever been there. He turned back to Steve and said, "What the hell's wrong with you?"

"Ask him," Steve said. He stood up. His elbows burned where they'd hit the grass.

"You're friends," Casey said.

Spinelli wiped his hands on the sides of his pants and said, "I guess things changed."

Casey said, "Haskins asking Jeannie out is what's changed. You guys ain't—"

His mouth dropped open. He let out a laugh, pointed past the tennis court and called out, "Get a load of that!"

A kid with a white buzz cut was stumbling down the sidewalk, looking behind him every few steps. A skinny woman staggered after him, her legs stiff, one hand stretched out in front of her trying to grab the boy. An old black Chevy crawled along behind the woman, a snot-faced girl hanging out the window, a guy in work clothes hunched over the steering wheel watching the woman who was chasing the boy.

"It's a goddamn hobo parade," Casey whispered.

The younger boys crept out of the darkness and stood by the

picnic table, Chuck with half a cigarette still hanging from his mouth. Omsted stayed on his swing, his back to the others, staring at the ground.

Chuck said, "That's Evelyn Schmidt."

"The cancer woman?" Steve whispered.

Rusch pointed to the corner and said, "That's their house."

Steve said, "No wonder she's got cancer. She's so skinny she can hardly walk."

"She didn't get cancer from being skinny," Chuck said. "She got it from not staying home with her kids."

"What are you? A fucking doctor?"

"My mom used to know her."

"No wonder you're a runt. You probably got cancer yourself."

"Shhh!" Casey said and pointed over at the kid on the sidewalk.

The kid was staring into the park, his eyes boring holes through the night. Evelyn staggered up behind him and grabbed him. He broke away and ran off. Evelyn lost her balance and fell to the ground.

The girl shouted, "Mamma!"

The Chevy jerked to a halt.

The boy stopped at the corner, looked at his mother on the ground, then turned and ran across the street into the beat-up house on the corner.

The girl and the man hopped out of the car. The girl got to Evelyn first, screamed "Mamma!" and tried to pull her upright. The man jumped the curb, pushed the girl away and knelt over Evelyn. The girl landed on her ass on the sidewalk and sat there bawling. In the house on the corner, an upstairs window opened and the boy's white head popped out.

Evelyn retched and gagged. The man got his head under her

arm and pulled her to her feet. He yelled at the girl, who jumped up, ran to the car and shut the doors. The guy dragged Evelyn down the sidewalk, under the street light, and into their yard.

Evelyn broke away from him when they got to the porch. She caught herself on the railing, lowered herself to the bottom step, and sat staring at the park. The girl came into the yard. The man barked at her and stormed into the house; she followed him, touching her mother's shoulder as she passed her on the steps. A light went on inside; the old guy was at the window talking on the phone.

Steve said, "She oughtta be in the hospital."

"Maybe she don't want to die in the hospital," Spinelli said. He was leaning against the shack, hands in his pockets, a cigarette hanging from the corner of his mouth.

"Why not? That's what they build 'em for."

Casey said, "Ain't gonna hurt nothing, letting her die the way she wants."

"She's got cancer. It ain't none of her business what she wants." Steve climbed onto the picnic table, and sat there staring at Evelyn.

Across the street, the girl came out of the house carrying a big white bowl and sat down on the steps next to Evelyn.

Rusch put his foot on Chuck's shoulder and knocked him over. "Look at this dumb shit. He's sick."

"I am not," Chuck said. He sat up and hunched against the tree.

"Then have a cigarette."

"I already had one."

Rusch flipped open his Marlboros and said, "Take another one or I'll kick your ass."

Down the block, the porch light at Putzie's house blinked on.

The kids from the station wagon came screaming off the porch and down the street towards the corner, a taller kid chasing after them with a sheet over his head.

Evelyn turned her head at the noise, then pulled herself up, holding tight to the railing. The smallest girl saw Evelyn and froze; a square-headed boy bumped into her. The tall kid saw Evelyn and pulled the sheet off his head. The others ran back and hid behind him.

The skinny guy, the fat woman, and Putzie's mother came out on the porch, with Putzie's brother trailing behind. The guy saw Evelyn and hopped off the porch, waving his hands at the kids, herding them towards the car. Putzie's brother hid behind his mother's dress.

Evelyn grabbed the candy bowl and stumbled across her front yard into the street. "You kids—"

The kids screamed and ran for the car, except for the little girl who stood in the street, looking into her bag. The skinny guy was yelling through the car window as the tall kid helped the others pile in.

"We still have candy," Evelyn said.

The little girl came down the street towards her.

The fat woman yelled, "Deena, no!"

The little girl kept walking.

Evelyn lurched forward, holding out the bowl. The fat woman jumped off the porch. The tall kid turned away from the station wagon hollering, "Deena, don't!"

Evelyn and the girl met in the street. The girl held her bag up and Evelyn took a handful of candy from the bowl and dropped it into her bag.

The fat woman reached them as the candy dropped and snatched the bag away. The little girl grabbed for it. The fat woman pushed

her away yelling, "No!" The tall kid scooped the girl up from behind and carried her squirming to the car. She stretched her arms
out over his shoulders, yelling for her candy. The fat woman tipped
the bag upside down, dumping the candy into the street, and the
girl screamed like she'd been stabbed. The tall kid pushed her into
the back seat of the station wagon and climbed in after her. The
other kids stuck their heads out of the windows, looking at the
pile of candy in the street.

The car pulled up next to the fat woman, who climbed in and
reached into the back seat to slap the girl across the face. The
screaming stopped. The car swerved around Evelyn and took off
down Ontario Street. Putzie's mother and brother went back in
the house.

Evelyn stood alone like a ghost in the road. The bowl in her
arms fell to the pavement and smashed. She reached after it, tottered and fell.

Her daughter screamed, "Mama!" and ran down the steps.

The man bolted from the house, passing the girl before she
reached the sidewalk. He dropped to his knees behind Evelyn and
held her shoulders as she lay choking in the road. The girl shoved
her fist in her mouth and stood at the curb bawling. The boy in
the upstairs window pulled his head back inside when his father
looked around.

When Evelyn stopped gasping, the man dragged her back to
the porch, lowered her to the bottom step, and sat down beside
her. Her cough rattled across the park like winter sleet. The boy
leaned out of the upstairs window again to watch what was happening on the steps.

Chuck finished the cigarette.

Rusch stuck his Marlboros in Chuck's face and said, "Take
another one."

Chuck pushed the pack away, turned and pressed his forehead against a tree.

Carner said, "Holy shit, he is sick."

"Smoke this. You'll feel better." Rusch stuck another cigarette between Chuck's lips.

"I ain't sick." Chuck knocked the cigarette out of his mouth and staggered towards the swing set.

Rusch fell against the tree laughing.

Carner blocked Chuck's path, held out a cigarette and said, "Smoke it, asshole."

"You go to hell!" Chuck hollered.

Steve bounded from the table over to the swings, yanked Chuck by his jacket collar and said, "I told you little bastards to shut up." He threw Chuck back against the tree.

Carner giggled and headed for the tree, still holding the cigarette.

Steve said, "If I have to tell you guys again, you'll be digging your heads out of your asses."

Chuck pushed himself off from the tree and ran for the street. Steve sprinted after him, pulled him to the ground, and grabbed him by the hair. "Where you think you're going, runt?"

"Home."

"Think again." Steve stood up, pulling Chuck to his feet.

Omsted said, "Who are you now? God?"

"One of you assholes ratted us out already tonight, Spuds. It ain't gonna happen again." Steve dragged Chuck back to the tree.

Chuck yelled, "I don't have to stay here if I don't want to!"

Steve shook him by the hair. "You do what I tell you or I'll kick your ass! You hear me? I'll kick your goddamn ass!" He shoved Chuck in the direction of Rusch and Carner. "Sit over there with the rest of the assholes."

Chuck staggered forward, head down, eyes closed.

Carner put his foot out, and Chuck tripped and fell across Rusch's legs.

"What a putz," Rusch said.

Chuck got to his knees, gagged once, and threw up in Rusch's lap.

Carner jumped up squealing and ran to the far side of the swing set.

Rusch yelled, "Jesus Christ!" and hopped up and down, trying to shake off the vomit.

Chuck crawled to the tree and put his head against it. Rusch scraped off the vomit with his hand and flung it at Chuck, yelling, "I should make you eat this, you little freak!"

The vomit hit Chuck in the face. He closed his eyes and gagged again but didn't throw up.

Spinelli came up next to Steve.

"What?" Steve said.

"Let him go. He's sick."

"He ain't so sick he can't rat on us."

Spinelli said, "You're nuts," and went back to the picnic table.

"You think I'm so nuts, maybe you're the one should go home."

Spinelli let his breath out, looked up at the sky, then down at Steve, and said, "Yeah, maybe I should." He pulled his bicycle out from under the picnic table.

Casey sat up in the grass and said, "Spinelli, don't be an asshole."

Spinelli said, "Fuck off, Casey," and climbed onto his bike.

"Let him go," Steve said. "I ain't so stupid I need help from a backstabbing coward."

Spinelli let his bicycle drop and came after Steve, hollering, "You want to know what's stupid?"

Casey said, "Spinelli, don't—"

"This whole fuckin' thing is stupid!" Spinelli poked Steve in the shoulder with two fingers. "You thinking Putzie was gonna believe your note was from Jeannie. *That* was stupid!"

"That was my idea," Casey said.

Spinelli poked Steve again. "Thinking Jeannie wouldn't dump you when she found out you were too dumb to stay on the team. *That* was stupid—"

Steve cried out and lunged forward, head lowered, slamming his shoulder into Spinelli's chest. Spinelli stumbled back and came up with his fists raised. "You asked for it, asshole."

He moved in low and punched Steve in the stomach, knocking him into the grass.

Before Steve could get his wind back, Casey was standing between them pointing to the corner. "Look, goddamn it," he whispered. "Look at that!"

Putzie Van Vonderan was standing under the streetlight by the tennis court, one hand over his eyes, peering into the park.

Steve rolled onto his stomach, hissing, "Everybody down!"

Casey and Spinelli dropped beside Steve. Rusch and Carner crawled towards them, leaving Chuck clinging to the tree. Omsted stopped swinging; the chains gave a dying creak.

Putzie turned in the direction of the noise. His ears stuck out from his head. His sweatshirt was too small, and his jeans were too big; they bunched up around the waist and bulged at the ankles. He dropped his hand from his eyes and stepped into the park.

Omsted started swinging again; the chains creaked in the dark. Steve motioned frantically for him to stop, but Spinelli whispered, "No. He thinks it's Jeannie. He really thinks it's Jeannie."

Putzie came towards the swing set, running his fingers through his hair, pushing it off his forehead.

Omsted's feet scraped the dirt; his swing creaked to a stop. Steve motioned for him to keep going. His brother gave him the finger.

Putzie said, "Jeannie?" He walked past the boys in the grass, tugging at the bottom of his sweatshirt, his eyes on the swing set. Casey, Spinelli, and Steve stood up quietly, making a wall behind him. Omsted stuck a cigarette in his mouth and flipped his lighter open with a click.

Putzie said, "Jeannie?" and stopped.

Rusch and Carner got to their feet.

Putzie took another step.

Omsted flicked the lighter. His face flared up orange in the dark.

Putzie stepped backwards.

"Hello, Putzie," Steve said.

Putzie spun around to look behind him, and froze.

Omsted got off his swing. The boys formed a circle around him.

Steve said, "What you doing in town, Putzie?"

"Maybe he's so stupid he doesn't know he's in town," Rusch said.

"Is that it, Putzie? You so stupid you wandered off your farm and don't even know it?"

Putzie curled his hands into fists; beads of sweat rolled out of his hair and down his forehead.

"Maybe he's so stupid he can't even talk," Omsted said.

"You too stupid to talk, Putzie?" Steve said and took a step closer. The rest of the circle moved in, too. Putzie made a grunting noise and pushed his arms out.

"Maybe you're so stupid all you can do is moo."

The others laughed.

"Moo for us, Putzie."

Behind Putzie, Carner said, "Moo." Putzie wheeled around to face him. Carner laughed. Then Rusch said, "Moo." Then Casey, then Spinelli, until they were all mooing and Putzie spun to face each of them in turn, the veins in his neck tight, his breath exploding from his nostrils.

Steve raised his hand and the mooing stopped. Leaves rustled all around them.

"What're you doing in the park, Putzie?"

Putzie looked around the circle.

"Answer me!" Steve yelled.

Putzie's eyes went back to Steve. He said, "I was walking."

Steve yelled, "Don't lie to me!" and grabbed the front of Putzie's sweatshirt. The circle closed in. Putzie's eyes rolled in his head, trying to see where he couldn't.

"You came here looking for somebody. Who were you looking for, Putzie?"

"My dog," Putzie said.

"It was Jeannie Erickson, you lying son of a bitch! You came looking for Jeannie!"

Putzie shook his head violently.

"We know about the note, Putzie," Steve said.

Putzie turned his face away.

"She sent you a note saying she was gonna be here."

"It was a joke," Putzie said.

"Why would she play a joke on you, Putzie?" Steve twisted the sweatshirt into a knot around Putzie's throat and yelled, "Is it because she thinks you're a piece of shit?"

The guys in the circle laughed.

"She don't think I'm shit!"

"She thinks you're shit, Putzie. She wouldn't have sent you that note if she didn't think you were shit."

"She did it so I'd leave her alone. She's already got a boyfriend."

"No kidding," Steve said. He shoved Putzie backward, so he stumbled into Spinelli. Spinelli caught Putzie's arms and yanked them behind his back.

Steve walked up to Putzie, smiling. Putzie turned his face away. Casey grabbed him by the hair and turned him back to face Steve.

"Who's her boyfriend, Putzie?" Steve said.

Rusch laughed. Carner giggled.

Spinelli twisted Putzie's arms. "Answer the man."

Steve yelled, "Who's her fucking boyfriend, Putzie?"

"Tim Haskins," Putzie mumbled.

Carner and Rusch stopped laughing.

Steve let go of Putzie's shirt.

Spinelli said, "Hit him."

Steve yelled, "She ain't going with Tim Haskins, you piece of shit. She's going with me." He drove his fist into Putzie's stomach.

Putzie's breath came out with a *huh* and he fell to his knees. Steve stepped back, rubbing his fist with his other hand. Putzie tried to get up but fell on his face in the dirt.

"Pick him up."

Rusch and Spinelli pulled Putzie to his feet. Putzie tried to shake them off but Rusch kicked his legs out from under him. Putzie stopped struggling and hung like a rag doll between Rusch and Spinelli.

Steve said, "Look at me, Putzie."

"Look at him, asshole," Omsted said and grabbed Putzie by the hair.

"You know how long I been going with Jeannie Erickson?"

Putzie shook his head, his eyes wide.

"Four years," Steve said. He stuck his face closer to Putzie's and yelled, "Four goddamn years!"

Omsted yanked Putzie's head back. Putzie retched and spit rolled down his chin.

"And after four goddamn years some fucking farmer thinks he can come into town and say she don't belong to me anymore?"

Putzie said, "I didn't—"

"Don't lie to me, Putzie," Steve yelled. "You said it right here!"

"Deck him," Spinelli said.

"Knock his teeth down his throat," Rusch said.

Steve put one hand behind Putzie's head as if he was cradling a baby and said, "You lied about my girlfriend, Putzie!"

Putzie yelled, "I didn't know!" then Steve's fist hit him in the face.

Steve started punching with both hands, landing blow after blow on Putzie's nose and mouth and eyes. When Putzie staggered, Rusch and Spinelli released him and Steve caught him in a headlock. He kept swinging as the boys around him hollered for him to knock Putzie's teeth out, pound his face in, rip his head off, break his neck.

Across the street, the man from the corner house peered into the park. He yelled, "You kids over there, I'm calling the police!" He looked at Evelyn, who was sitting on the steps with her head pressed against the rails, pointed at the little girl like he was giving an order, then went into the house. When the door closed, Evelyn stood up, pushed herself off the railing, and staggered towards the park.

Putzie finally wrenched himself out of the headlock and looked around for a way out of the circle. He tried to make a run past Casey, but Casey shoved him back into Steve and fell down laughing. Steve grabbed Putzie by the shoulder. Putzie whipped around with his fists raised and caught Steve on the chin, knocking him down. Spinelli and Rusch jumped into the circle and grabbed Putzie's arms.

Steve got to his feet and said, "You're one stupid son of a bitch, you know that, farmer?"

Putzie said, "I didn't do anything to you."

"When I get through with you, you're gonna wish you'd killed me."

Steve slammed his fist into Putzie's stomach. Putzie doubled over; Spinelli and Rusch yanked him upright again.

"Whose girlfriend is she now, asshole?" Steve said, and punched Putzie in the stomach.

Putzie tried to double up but couldn't.

"Tell me she's going with Haskins now, you stupid fucking farmer!" Steve shouted and hit him again.

Putzie yelled, "I saw—"

"You didn't see shit!" Steve smashed his fist into Putzie's face.

Putzie's head flew back in a spray of red. He screamed at Steve through busted lips, "I saw 'em kissing by the gym!"

Steve's fist froze in the air.

The boys in the circle stopped breathing.

Putzie sucked air through his bleeding nose.

"Let go of him," Steve said.

Spinelli and Rusch gave Putzie a shove towards Steve. Putzie staggered two steps forward and stopped. Steve put a hand on Putzie's shoulder, smiled, and brought his knee up hard into Putzie's crotch. "You lying son of a bitch!" he shrieked.

Putzie went down and Steve moved in, kicking. Putzie clawed at the air. The noises he made could have been words, but they were drowned out by the boys yelling, "Kill him!"

Putzie clawed his way to his knees, screamed at Steve and spit out a tooth. He scrambled after it, but Steve kicked him again and he fell back down.

Steve said, "Lie to us now, you stupid farmer."

"Nod stubid," Putzie mumbled.

"You're stupid, Putzie! You're as stupid as your goddamn headless father!"

Putzie forced his head up out of the dirt and shrieked, "S'nod stubid!"

"Even a farmer's gotta be a moron to go through his own goddamn threshing machine!" Steve yelled.

Putzie came up screaming, spraying blood in Steve's face. Steve jumped back, but Putzie was already on him, his big hands on Steve's throat. He barely heard Evelyn cry "Stop it! All of you," as she staggered across the street towards them.

Putzie's fist hit him full on the jaw, again and again, until there was a crack, and stars, and then the world went dark.

Steve woke up on the ground at the center of the circle. Putzie was beyond them, backing his way out of the park. As Steve climbed to his feet, pain sliced through his head. He screamed, his jaw hanging loose to one side.

Spinelli came towards him, hands outstretched. Steve screamed, "Keep away from me!" but his mouth couldn't shape the words right. He put his hand up to push his jaw back into place, but the pain made him scream again.

Spinelli turned and yelled, "Grab the son of a bitch!"

Putzie took off running but Rusch tackled him. They landed in the dirt in front of Evelyn who had gotten tangled up in the swings.

Rusch jumped up. He yelled, "You fucking farmer!" and stomped on Putzie's back. Evelyn screamed. Then Casey, Spinelli, and Carner piled in on Putzie, too. Omsted arrived and kicked at Putzie with his heels, yelling, "Go for his head!"

Putzie groaned and puked each time someone jumped on him. Evelyn clung to the chain of a swing, yelling between coughs for the boys to stop.

Steve backed away into the dark. He bumped into the picnic table, turned on it, and kicked it. Pain shot up his leg and through his back to his jaw, making him grab his jaw again and scream. He stumbled on through dirty leaves, kicking up a tornado of dirt and dust that made him close his eyes, so that he ran into a group of wooden stakes stuck in the ground. Steve swung at them, cursed when they bounced back and gave him splinters, cursed Casey for tearing them off the shack and almost killing him earlier. Then he pulled one of them from the ground, raised it over his shoulder, and lurched back towards the others.

Rusch was holding Putzie by the hair and jumping on his back. The rest of them surrounded the runt, who was kneeling under the tree, his arms wrapped around it, shaking his head. Omsted was pointing at Putzie and yelling in a cracked voice, "Get over here and kick him. Now!"

Chuck got up. Spinelli yelled, "Faster!" Chuck hung back, but Omsted shoved him forward, yelling "Now!"

Chuck closed his eyes and kicked Putzie in the head. Then he opened them and kicked him again. And then they were all on him, kicking and jumping, laughing and yelling.

Across the street, the man came out of the corner house and ran into the park, the little girl straggling after him. The white-haired boy hung out the upstairs window calling for his ma to come back.

Evelyn threw herself off the swings and had staggered halfway to the boys when Steve threw himself forward. "Let go of him!" he hollered.

The boys looked up, two rows of bloody faces with Putzie crawling between them like a bug down an aisle, and Evelyn trying to stay upright at the other end. Steve lifted the jagged board off his shoulder. Putzie crawled towards Evelyn, his arms and legs wiggling faster than his body could go. Spinelli reached into the aisle to grab the board away, but Steve rushed past him and plunged the spear into Putzie's back.

Putzie shuddered and shrieked but kept on pulling himself down the aisle, the spear swaying from side to side, to where Evelyn stood tottering, her hands stretched out towards him. He grabbed her wrists, pulling her down as he pulled himself up.

Evelyn fell to her knees under Putzie's weight. She tried to stand and lift him up with her, but he screamed and she sank back, let him pull himself onto her, the board sticking out of his back like a giant needle. He had crawled up to her shoulders before his legs gave out. She held him then, staggering under his weight, until what was left of him raised his head and looked into her face.

His eyes bugged out and his head snapped back. His hands flailed against her chest. His legs convulsed as if he was trying to run away. Evelyn cried at him to stop moving and held him against her as she tried to pull the spear from his back. She couldn't reach, and then Putzie's hands found her face and clawed at it. "Noooo!" he moaned. Then he howled, "Let go of me" so loud it seemed to echo around the town.

Evelyn let go as Putzie shoved himself away from her. He staggered backward until the end of the board caught in the dirt behind him. Spinelli put his hands over his eyes. Evelyn covered her mouth. Putzie went down backward onto the board, shrieking and waving his arms until its point came through his chest and splattered Evelyn with blood and black matter. Putzie stopped screaming then. He slid to the ground gurgling, the spear running through him. Then everything was quiet, except for Evelyn, who tottered around in circles, sobbing and wiping blood from her dress.

"Oh, Jesus Christ," Carner said.

Spinelli said, "Shut the fuck up."

Chuck backed up against a tree and pushed at it with his hands and feet like he was trying to climb it backwards.

Spinelli pointed a finger at Steve and said, "He was the only one here."

Steve shook his head.

Spinelli turned to the other boys and jabbed his finger at each of them. "No matter what happens, we were not here. He was the only one."

Carner moaned, "Oh, Jesus Christ. Oh, Jesus Christ."

"I told you to shut up!" Spinelli said and backhanded Carner, who started to cry.

Spinelli turned to Rusch and said, "Get him out of here."

A siren wailed once downtown and stopped.

The man and the girl ran across the tennis court, the man yelling, "Stay where you are! I called the police!"

The boys scattered and ran. Spinelli dashed for his bike. Casey sprinted for the woods.

Rusch grabbed Carner and Chuck and pushed them towards Ontario Street. Omsted followed them. They turned their heads away as they raced past the man running toward Evelyn. As they headed down Ontario and disappeared into the shadows in the middle of the block, Carner was crying that the nuns would figure it out, you couldn't hide from the nuns. Then his voice faded.

Steve stayed where he was, holding his face, staring at the man running towards him, but the man stopped when he reached Evelyn. She fell to her hands and knees and vomited blood.

A siren sounded close by.

Footsteps headed down Ontario and Omsted ran back into the park.

Somewhere up the hill, Casey called out, "Come on."

Omsted grabbed Steve by the arm, hissing, "You gotta get out of here! Dad'll kill you for this!" Steve shoved his brother away and turned up the hill to where Casey was still calling. Omsted tried to drag him towards the corner instead. "Not that way! The woods is the first place they'll look."

The girl had edged her way around her father and was looking from her mother to Putzie to Steve. The siren wailed again and red lights came flashing down Ontario. Casey hollered from the woods. Steve shook off his brother and punched him in the nose when he tried to grab him again. Omsted staggered backward, his hand to his face, and stared at Steve over his bloody fingers without saying anything.

Red lights sliced across the tennis court.

Steve turned and ran out of the park and into the night.

He ran up the hill, dodging trees that jumped up in front of him, swatting at kicked-up leaves that cut at his eyes like knives. Then the red lights were after him, bloody fingers reaching up to pluck him out of the park. They covered the hill. Across the street there were houses hidden away in the dark. He ran towards them.

A long red finger flicked across the street ahead of him. He ducked under it, stumbled and fell. He scrambled up the curb and across a front yard, then dove for a clump of bushes. But a dog on a chain jumped out snarling and Steve had to crawl under the lights to the next house. Red lights flashed everywhere. He struggled through a pile of molding leaves, fought past a tangle of broken bushes, and wriggled under a porch.

The siren wailed to a stop nearby. The red lights chased the darkness across the lawn and swept under the edge of the porch. Steve slid backward, pulled his knees to his chest to make himself smaller. A cop's voice crackled over a radio and made him jump. Something scurried under the porch. He caught his breath and waited.

From the wall behind him something like a leaf fell on his neck, then slid down his back like a spider. He reached down the back of his jacket, but more things slid down his neck. He scrambled forward but the red light was waiting for him. He moved back and hit the wall. Something scurried under the porch again. He kicked at it. His foot hit something, a rock or a rat, and he kicked again, and swore—at the animal that was after him, at the spiders crawling down his neck, at the light sneaking under the porch. His breath caught in his throat, and when he opened his mouth to let it out he started to cry, and couldn't stop. He curled himself into a ball, pushed his fists into his eyes, and cursed, kicking at things in the dark, until he was crying too hard to curse any more.

5

CRACK THE WHIP

Omsted burst out of the dark at the top of the hill and skidded to a halt under the streetlight that hung over the intersection. Gasping for air, he hissed for the others to stop. Rusch stumbled and fell panting to the curb. Carner spun in circles, whining, "Jesus Christ! Oh, Jesus Christ!" Omsted growled at him to shut up. Chuck crested the hill and stopped at the edge of the circle of light. He leaned against a fire hydrant, watching.

A half mile down the hill, a cop car wailed up George Street and turned onto Ontario, the siren cutting off as it came to a halt.

Omsted's head snapped up. Rusch got to his feet. Carner ran to the edge of the hill, whimpering and pulling the fingers of one hand with the fingers of the other. Another cop car sped down Ontario towards the park, where the tree tops glowed with flickering lights.

Carner backed up and grabbed Omsted. "They're gonna come up here! That little girl will tell 'em where we are!"

"She was looking at Putzie. She didn't even know we were there." Omsted shoved Carner away.

Another siren. Rusch threw himself back down and pounded his fist against the curb, muttering, "Shit! Shit! Shit!"

Carner came up behind Omsted, still wringing his hands. "What if Spinelli tells 'em we were there?"

Omsted was watching Rusch and frowning. He said, "Spinelli ain't telling anybody we were there because he ain't telling anybody *he* was there."

"What if they catch Steve? If Steve tells 'em Spinelli was there, Spinelli could rat us out."

Omsted grabbed Carner by the throat and slammed him against a phone pole. "My brother's not a squealer," he snarled.

Carner clawed at the hands on his throat.

"You got me?"

Carner nodded. Omsted let him go. Carner sank to the ground coughing.

Another siren blared in the dark. Rusch jumped off the curb. He ran his hands through his hair and said, "We gotta move."

"We can cut down Webster and circle back to the woods," Omsted said.

Chuck stood up, shaking his head.

"What?" Rusch said.

Omsted said, "We gotta make sure Spinelli and Casey found Steve."

"Spinelli was home in bed before Putzie hit the ground," Rusch said.

Omsted stared down Webster, biting his lip. "We better go get him ourselves then," he said and headed towards the park without looking back.

"Leave him, Omsted," Rusch yelled. "He ain't your problem!"

Omsted turned back. "He's my brother, asshole!"

"You think he wouldn't turn on you if he had to?"

"He wouldn't."

"He already did," Chuck said. He came into the intersection and stood next to Rusch.

Rusch took a cigarette out of his pocket, twirled it in his fingers, and brought it towards his mouth.

Omsted said, "You don't know what the hell you're talking about."

"He told Putzie's mother you were Omsted when she came to the park," Chuck said.

Rusch's fingers twitched, snapping his cigarette in two.

Omsted turned away muttering.

A siren split the dark, making them jump.

Carner pointed at Omsted. "She saw what you looked like! She can tell the cops you were there!"

Omsted yelled, "Being there and killing Putzie are two different things!"

"Maybe not to the cops!"

Rusch pulled his fingers through his hair. He sucker punched the air and screamed "Shit!"

Carner grabbed Rusch's arm and said, "We gotta go back."

"Are you nuts?" Rusch cried.

"We gotta go back and tell 'em what happened." Carner's voice cracked. He pulled on the sleeve of Rusch's sweatshirt. "We gotta go back and tell 'em ourselves. That's the only way they're gonna believe us."

"You ain't going back and telling 'em shit," Omsted said.

Carner said, "We could go to jail—"

"You think we're turning my brother over to the cops just cause you're a piss-pants?"

"He *killed* somebody!" Carner yelled.

Rusch yanked his arm out of Carner's grip and punched him on the side of the head. Carner yelped and put his hand to his ear. Rusch grabbed him by the hair and swung him around to face Omsted.

"Nobody killed anybody. You hear me?" Omsted said.

Carner spluttered, "Steve killed Putzie. I saw him."

"It was an accident!" Omsted shouted and drove his fist into Carner's stomach. Carner retched, and his head fell forward. Rusch yanked him back by his hair.

Omsted said, "Listen to me good, asshole. There's four of us here, counting you, and three of us are saying we weren't at the park. Are you calling us liars?"

Carner sniveled, and tried to shake his head.

"Say it."

Rusch gave Carner's hair a twist and said, "Say it, asshole."

Carner's eyes turned sideways like he was trying to see Rusch. He whimpered once and mumbled, "We were never in the park."

Rusch let go of his hair and shoved him away. Carner stumbled a few steps and stood with his back to them. He tried to cover his sobs by holding his breath.

Chuck came into the light, his hands in his jacket pockets. He looked at Omsted and said, "We gotta pick a place to say we were, some place they can't prove if we were or not."

Carner wheeled around. "There ain't any such place."

Rusch said, "My old lady ain't home. We can go to my place and say we been there for hours." He turned his back to Carner and made an okay sign at Chuck.

"Only we won't really go there," Chuck said. "That way the neighbors won't see us going in or out."

"Then where *are* we supposed to go?" Carner whined.

"Home," Chuck said.

They stood facing each other in a circle. Carner started sniveling again.

Omsted nodded and said, "Let's go then."

Omsted and Rusch began walking with Chuck between them. Carner dragged behind. Omsted pointed at him over his shoulder and said, "In front of us. Now."

They waited until Carner got in front of them and then followed him, walking right on his heels.

The road to their houses was off Webster, near the woods uphill from Legion Park. From a block away the woods jumped out at them, red and black shadows of trees swelling and shrinking in the flashing lights from below. The cops' radios crackled through the trees and into the street like live wires. Across from the woods, a frosted streetlight on a vine-covered pole marked the entrance to their neighborhood.

A siren moaned through the woods then died, and a cop car screeched to a halt at the corner, lights flashing.

Carner whined.

Rusch swore.

Omsted hissed, "They ain't looking for us!"

The car turned away from them onto Webster.

Carner whined, "They're gonna get us alone and start asking us things."

"We were at Rusch's house," Omsted said.

"One of us'll crack and tell the truth. We'll all look like liars then."

"If anyone cracks, it'll be you," Rusch said.

Carner pointed at Chuck and said, "What about him? You said he was a baby."

"How come you're doing all the crying then?" Chuck said.

Carner snapped, "Maybe 'cause I'm smart!"

"You're doing a good job of hiding it," Chuck said.

Rusch and Omsted laughed.

"I'm smarter than you! I ain't going to jail just because my friends are morons!" Carner shouted, and took off running.

Rusch quickly caught up with him, but Carner stuck his foot out and Rusch tripped and fell. Omsted and Chuck ran after Carner, but Omsted got a stitch after half a block and Chuck ran on alone. He caught up with Carner at the edge of the woods.

The boys crashed into the tangle without slowing down. Carner turned and spat as Chuck stretched out a hand and grabbed the neck of Carner's sweatshirt. The spit flashed up red between them and hit Chuck in the face. Chuck kept his grip and Carner lost his balance. They both tumbled into a pile of leaves.

Leaves exploded cold and black around them, the dust catching in their throats. When it cleared, Chuck was on top of Carner, knees pinning his chest, his hand flashing high and red in the air.

"They don't even like you!" Carner screamed.

Chuck's fist froze.

"They made you smoke cigarettes and laughed at you!"

Chuck let his fist drop. A red light swept over them. Carner's face glistened with tears and snot.

"We don't have to get caught," Carner said.

Omsted staggered into the woods, Rusch panting behind him. "Where is he?"

"Right here," Chuck said. He stood up, pulling Carner to his knees.

Down the hill in the park, cops scrambled amid the spinning red lights of their circled cars, pointing, shouting, forming huddles, breaking apart. Two of the cars had their spotlights turned on Putzie's body. On the corner, near the tennis court, Putzie's mother strained to try and escape the cops holding on to her arms, shoulders, and waist, her mouth stretched wide in a scream no one could hear. Beyond the park, faces filled the porches along Ontario Street like open-mouthed and quiet ghosts.

"Get up," Omsted said.

Carner whimpered and tried to stand.

Rusch said, "Now!" and yanked Carner to his feet.

Two ambulances screamed down Ontario and into the park. One of them stopped next to Putzie and two men jumped out. As they approached the body, their hands went to their mouths. The other ambulance stopped close to Evelyn. The doors flew open and two men jumped out. Evelyn backed away from them, waving her arms and wailing, "No!" Her husband came out of the darkness and caught hold of her, his face flashing up red in the night.

Evelyn's daughter started to bawl; a cop picked her up and held her. Her brother leaned out of his upstairs window and howled "Mama!" like a dog. Evelyn kicked out at the ambulance men as they came towards her and they quickly jumped back. Her husband grabbed her around the waist, hoisted her off the ground and into the back of the ambulance. He climbed in after her and the ambulance guys slammed the doors.

Carner ducked suddenly, breaking Rusch's grip on his shirt. "You son of a bitch," Rusch said and grabbed him by the back of the neck. Carner screamed like an animal.

A cop near Putzie clicked his flashlight on and shone it into the woods. The boys froze, Carner hanging like a dead bird in Rusch's grip.

"He saw us," Chuck said.

Omsted said, "Everybody out of here," and they ran, Rusch pushing Carner ahead of him, out of the woods, away from the flashing lights.

They ran across Webster Street and into their subdivision, but instead of turning down his own street, Carner kept going straight. He didn't stop until he came to the end of the road, three empty blocks past the last houses. A backhoe and a bulldozer loomed at the end of the road, where builders had started to dig the foundations of another new house. So far they'd only made a long trench, as deep as a basement and no wider than a car; in the moonlight it looked like a bottomless pit.

Carner skidded to a stop at the edge of the pit and spun to the right, but the others were already there, trapping him with his back to the black pit. "Stay away from me," he pleaded.

Rusch took a step towards him. Carner screamed and almost lost his balance. His cry spread across the fields and echoed off the ledge, a high rock cliff the glaciers had carved, which cut the town off from the rest of the world, and whose narrow top was dotted like a castle wall with the houses of the town's mayor, doctors, and lawyers.

Omsted stepped in front of Rusch, folded his arms, and said to Carner, "You ready to listen now?"

"I hope you get caught."

"If we get caught you get caught. We'll tell 'em *you* did it."

"I'll tell 'em the truth!"

"You might not get the chance."

Omsted nodded over his shoulder to Rusch. Rusch gave a low laugh and moved forward, slamming his fist into his palm. Carner edged away along the side of the pit, whimpering.

"You still want to tell the truth?"

"You go to hell."

"Go ahead," Omsted said to Rusch. He turned his back on Carner, put his arm around Chuck and led him away from the pit.

Chuck ducked away and turned back to watch Carner and

Rusch. Carner was skirting the pit; Rusch was blocking him, hands out, as if they were playing basketball, only Carner was sniveling, then sobbing as they played.

"You don't have to see this."

"Neither do you," Chuck said.

The boys continued their basketball game, Rusch's breathing almost drowning out Carner's sobs. Behind them, at the top of the black ledge, a light came on outside one of the houses and soon afterward a pair of headlights began to make its way down the side of the ledge. It was the doctor they called out when people died in car crashes.

Rusch looked up when he noticed the distant headlights. Carner lowered his head and tried to rush past him but Rusch caught him by the shoulders and sent him sprawling backwards.

Carner waved his arms like a bird flapping its wings, and tried to keep his balance at the edge of the hole. He stared accusingly at the others for a few long seconds then fell backwards into the pit with a whine that was cut off by a thud.

Rusch laughed and slapped his thigh. "He fell in the friggin' hole!"

Omsted told him to shut up. "He might be dead. Did you think of that?"

Rusch stopped laughing and stepped to the edge of the pit.

"It's not deep enough," Chuck said.

Omsted and Rusch looked back at him.

Chuck came forward and looked down into the darkness. "It's about eight feet. The only way the fall could kill him is if he fell on his head and broke his neck."

Rusch looked into the pit, and back to Chuck, his eyes wild with fear. His voice cracked. "He could've broke his neck?"

Omsted stared down and muttered, "He ain't crying."

"He *must've* fell on his head," Rusch gabbled. "You know he'd be crying if he didn't fall on his head."

"He didn't fall on his head," Chuck said.

"How the hell would you know?" Rusch shrieked.

Up on the ledge, lights at the mayor's house suddenly gleamed like fireflies. A few seconds later, lights blazed up at his brother's house next door, drowning out the mayor's lights. The mayor's brother was the district something, but Chuck's dad always called him the shyster. Soon two more pairs of headlights followed the doctor's, tracing a winding path down the ledge.

"I saw the way he fell," Chuck said. "He didn't go down head first. He fell on his ass."

A whimper came from the bottom of the pit, then a thin cry. "Rusch?"

Rusch turned back to the pit. Chuck put a hand up to shush him. Omsted saw it and put a hand on Rusch's shoulder to silence him.

Rusch mouthed, "What?"

"Omsted!" Carner cried from the pit.

Omsted looked at Chuck. Chuck put his finger over his lips and walked to the edge of the hole. "They're not here," he said.

"Where are they?"

"They went to get a gun."

Carner's voice collapsed to a whimper. "Why?"

"They're gonna kill you."

Carner shrieked. A cloud of moldy, frozen dirt rose from the pit along with the panicked cry, as he tried to climb the frost-hardened wall of the pit.

"Shhhhh!" Chuck said and knelt down at the edge of the pit.

Carner fell silent.

"What are you gonna do if I let you out of here?"

"We gotta go to the cops," Carner whispered.

"You tell Rusch or Omsted that, they'll shoot your tongue right out of your mouth."

"We don't gotta tell 'em! We just gotta pretend to go along with them."

Chuck stood up.

"You gotta get me out of here," Carner yelled.

"I *am* going along with them."

Rusch looked over the edge of the pit and said, "But you ain't, Carner."

Carner's shrill voice fought its way up the side of the pit. "Rusch! Did you hear what he was trying to get me to do?"

Omsted stepped to the edge of the pit. "We heard everything, Carner."

"He said you'd gone."

"I lied," Chuck said, scooping up a clump of frozen dirt and dropping it into the pit. It sounded like gravel landing on cement.

"What are you doing?"

"Goodbye, asshole," Chuck said and dropped another handful of dirt.

"Rusch, help!"

"I'll help," Omsted said. He too picked up a handful of dirt and threw it into the pit.

Carner cried out as the clumps struck his head.

Rusch laughed and joined in.

Carner was babbling now. "You can't do this, you guys. You'll get caught, you know you will. Rusch—"

At the bottom of the ledge, the sets of headlights caught up with one other. The three cars turned onto the main road in procession. A sharp wind ripped across the field, tearing open the clouds and exposing the moon. The moon lit up the fields, picking out Carner cowering and babbling at the bottom of the hole, and revealing a huge pile of dirt beside the freshly dug pit.

Rusch laughed and bounded up the pile. He pushed the top of the mound into the pit, knocking Carner flat on his back. Carner squeaked as his breath was knocked out of him. Rusch yelled, "Let's bury the guy!" Chuck and Omsted raced up the pile and helped Rusch push more and more dirt into the pit.

Carner struggled to his hands and knees and fought to stand up.

"Omsted . . . they'll come looking for you first. When they find out about your brother they'll—"

A large clump of dirt hit his head and made him scream.

"First they'll have to find *you*," Omsted shouted and aimed a clump of dirt like a snowball at Carner's head.

"You're gonna kill me!"

"You're already dead," Chuck said. "We're just burying you."

Rusch and Omsted laughed and pelted Carner with frozen dirt balls. Chuck continued to scoop armfuls of dirt into the pit.

A cop car had come to the base of the ledge to meet the mayor and the others. It made a U-turn in the middle of the road, red lights flashing, and preceded them into town.

The dirt was piling up around Carner now and he could no longer keep his arms and legs free. He was stuck halfway down the pit and couldn't move.

"I won't tell anybody. You know I won't tell anybody! I'll tell 'em what you tell me to tell. Rusch, you gotta help me."

A dirt ball hit his head and exploded.

"Rusch, you can't kill me! I didn't do anything to you! I was gonna say you weren't even there!"

"You lying son of a bitch!" Rusch yelled and dropped to his knees to scoop more dirt into the pit. Omsted kneeled beside Rusch and Chuck and the three of them went to work in earnest, grunting and panting now, not laughing any more.

The dirt nearly covered Carner's chest; he was mumbling and whimpering, begging for help, his bursts of words becoming incoherent.

The cars moved down the winding road into town, close enough now for the boys to hear the tires crunching on the frosted pavement, and see the cop's flashing beams sweep high over the pit.

Carner called out to the light, a feeble call for help that even the boys could barely hear. Omsted stopped scooping long enough to pack a dirt ball and aim it at Carner's head. Carner strained his neck towards the light and called again. This time it was almost a shout.

The boys froze. Chuck said, "If they hear him—"

Omsted and Rusch stared at each other.

Chuck jumped into the pit, grabbed Carner's hair and pushed his head down until the earth around his throat made him choke. Rusch and Omsted scrambled into the pit behind Chuck.

"That ain't the police," Chuck said.

A white beam passed high overhead. Rusch and Omsted ducked. Carner twisted his head free and shouted, "Help!" even louder this time. Chuck pushed him down again and hissed, "That ain't the cops, asshole!"

Carner cried out once more. Rusch clamped his hand over Carner's mouth but Carner bit him. Rusch pulled his hand away and snarled, "That ain't the cops, you homo, that's your ma!"

Chuck yelled at Rusch to shut up.

"It's your ma with a friggin' flashlight," Rusch growled. "You call her over here and we'll have to kill her."

"Shut the fuck up!" Chuck hissed. "I'm handling this."

Rusch turned to Omsted but the beam passed overhead again and they both ducked.

Chuck said, "They can't see us. We're in a hole."

"You don't know that," Rusch said.

"Yes, I do!"

"Mama," Carner whimpered.

Chuck yanked Carner's head back. "Shut up!"

Carner whimpered again, louder this time, "Mama!"

"We gotta get him out of here," Chuck said.

"How?' Omsted's voice was shaky and thin.

"Dig!" Chuck shouted and began to claw at the earth around Carner's neck. Carner strained against the earth as if to help them but as soon as his throat was free he screamed "Maaamaaa!" so loud that his voice echoed off the ledge and across the fields.

The beam of light seemed to freeze above them as if trying to fix the scream in the clouds. The cars had come to a halt.

Omsted muttered, "Oh shit."

Now the white beam sliced the dark closer to the ground, then weaved back and forth above the hole. One of the drivers tapped his horn impatiently.

"You two get out of here," Chuck said.

Omsted whined, "How?'

"On your belly. Crawl! Don't stand up till you get to Elm Street."

Rusch and Omsted scuttled out of the pit and disappeared. The searching light came to rest a few feet above the hole. Carner stared at it and whispered, "Mama?"

Chuck grabbed Carner by the chin and looked straight into his eyes. "That ain't your mama."

Carner stared blankly back at Chuck and said, "Mama" again.

"That ain't your mama, it's the cops."

Carner's eyes focused.

"They'll dig you out of here."

"I want my mama."

The light jerked down closer to the pit.

Chuck grabbed Carner's chin and hissed, "Listen to me! The cops are coming to get you out of here. But I'm gonna be watching everything you do. You tell them one word of the truth about what happened tonight, and I'll kill your mama right in front of you."

"Don't kill my mama!"

"Shut up!"

Chuck could hear the parade of cars coming closer now.

"I'll chop her head off and I'll make you watch."

Carner blubbered.

"You understand me?"

Carner nodded violently.

Chuck shoved Carner away and scrambled out of the pit just before the cop car turned the corner and sent its headlights glaring down the long empty road. He crawled through long grass and cornfield skeletons until he reached Elm Street.

Rusch and Omsted were huddled in the shadows. They stood up when they saw Chuck come round the corner. Omsted was sniffling like he was getting a cold. Together they peered back down the long ledge road to where the cop was being pelted with dirt balls in the glare of his own headlights. Carner was wailing, "You're not going to kill my mama. Nobody's gonna kill my ma!"

Omsted whispered, "What if he tells?"

"He's gone nuts," Chuck said. "Nobody'd believe him even if he could remember what there was to tell."

Rusch laughed. He clapped Omsted on the shoulder and said, "So what did we watch on TV tonight?"

Omsted stared at him blankly, then mumbled, "*Creature Features*. We were at your house watching *Creature Features*."

"Change of plan," Chuck said quietly.

"What's wrong with our plan?" Rusch said.

"Your best friend has been missing all night and you were home watching TV?"

"That backstabbing coward ain't my friend."

"You don't know that yet."

A smile that was half sneer worked its way across Rusch's face. He poked Omsted in the stomach and said, "Come on, let's go look for the little bastard on George Street."

Omsted shoved his hands in his pockets, poked his chin at Chuck and said, "And where are you going to be?"

"Home in bed," Chuck said. "I don't even know the guy."

Rusch tightened his grip on Omsted's shoulder. Omsted let himself be led away.

"Make sure the cops see you," Chuck hissed after them.

Rusch winked at Chuck, then turned his back and guided Omsted into the lights of Elm Street. Chuck waited until their footsteps and voices faded; then he headed home.

His house was dark except for a light in the kitchen where his father was sitting at the table in his pajamas. He hadn't thought his father would wait up for him.

Chuck's bedroom was upstairs at the back, but there was no easy way to get to it without being seen. The drainpipe for the eaves was at the front of the house and didn't look like it would hold his weight. But he had to try it. It creaked as he shimmied up but didn't come loose. He clambered onto the roof with a thud, waited to make sure his father was coming to the front to check on the noise, and then made his way quietly up the slanted roof, moving slowly, the tiles scuffing his hands like sandpaper.

He crested the roof and held on to the chimney. Behind the house, at the end of the empty road, two cop cars lit up the pit. Three cops were now trying to pull Carner out of the dirt, but he was resisting, his cries loud enough that they carried faintly to Chuck's ears even at this distance. Behind them the ledge blocked any view of the world beyond.

It was an easy slide down to his bedroom window, but he realized now that he'd never be able to grab the sill as he slid past. He'd have to slide down to the eaves on his stomach, grab the gutter, and drop to the ground again. But he still wouldn't be inside, would still have to explain what he'd been doing tonight, and why he looked such a mess.

Chuck tried to think it through as fast as he could. If he could control his fall, maybe fold one leg under him as he dropped, he'd probably break it or something. Then he could tell his dad that a gang of high-school kids had beat him up a while back, and he'd had to drag himself home.

And once people found out what had happened tonight, they'd figure it was the same guys who killed Putzie.

Maybe.

He stood up slowly, bracing himself against the chimney, and turned around.

Below him was the hollow that held the town. The fancier houses above Webster were mostly dark now. Past Webster, the hill dropped sharply through Legion Park to downtown, where the last store lights were going out and the big red owl on the supermarket winked and went dark. Between downtown and the hill were the houses where they used to live, with snub-nosed pumpkins lit by stunted candles glowing on their porches.

Rusch and Omsted were walking down George Street calling Carner's name. Diablo Hockers worked his way up the other side of the street, stopping at each house that still had a pumpkin burning and punting it into the street. The park was deserted now except for a lone cop car, its lights picking out the brown patch of dirt where Putzie had died.

Another cop car drove slowly up George Street, where the older houses met the flats of downtown, shining its spotlight under porches and into the bushes. Rusch waved at the cop and the cop nodded back. Then the cop spotted Diablo getting ready to punt a pumpkin from the porch of a brick house. He turned his spotlight on Diablo, who strolled up to the car carrying the pumpkin under his arm. The cop stepped out of the car; the two of them argued over the roof. Diablo gesturing that the pumpkin was his, the cop indicating that Diablo should head back downtown.

The cop got back in his car and continued up the hill. Diablo waited till the cop turned onto Webster then hurled the pumpkin at the car. The pumpkin splattered against a tree and Diablo ran back down the hill. The impact scared up a pair of blackbirds, who flew from the branches, circled Chuck and the chimney, and glided off into the icy night. High in the sky, a plane soared, its lights blinking. Above the plane, the moon rode the clouds, looking down on the earth and up at the stars.

Chuck grabbed on to the peak of the roof, lay down on his stomach, released his grip, and let himself fall.

AUTHOR'S NOTE

The first drafts of *A Map of the Dark* were written in San Francisco after I had been away from De Pere for twelve years. When I returned, I discovered that even though my memories were extremely vivid, I had nevertheless made several geographical errors in depicting my home town. Most of these errors were corrected in subsequent drafts, but a few that were crucial to the flow of the story remain. Also, while De Pere the place is very real, the story of *A Map of the Dark* is entirely of my invention, and its characters and events are fictitious.

FICTION FROM VERSE CHORUS PRESS

The Last Rock Star Book, or: Liz Phair, a Rant
Camden Joy
212 PAGES, PAPERBACK, $14.95

"I know of no one who writes with more passion and more soul."—*DAVE EGGERS*

Camden Joy's hero can't wrap up the quickie bio of rock star Liz Phair he's been commissioned to write. Instead, he finds himself recounting the troubled events of his own life. His ex-girlfriend (who might be the illegitimate daughter of dead Rolling Stone Brian Jones); Liz Phair (whom he's never met); and a mystery girl in an old newspaper photo all start to blur together in his mind. If he could just get closer to his subject, maybe he'd have a shot at the distinction he feels he deserves, before the assignment spins out of control . . . Hilarious and compelling, Joy's novel is both an engrossing read and a powerful meditation on celebrity and obsession.

Pretty Things
Susan Compo
204 PAGES, PAPERBACK, $16.95

"No one writes prose like Susan Compo. She's a complete LA original—elegant, wistful, funny . . . and not to be missed."—*SANDRA TSING LOH*

Booklist called Susan Compo "smart, sassy, and tough," while *Publishers Weekly* praised her "witty, unflinching prose." Compo's narrative voice—satirical and allusive—has been compared to Dorothy Parker's, and her characters display the same irresistible blend of smart-ass wit, despair, and whistling-in-the-dark bravado. *Pretty Things* offers both a sparkling portrait of a talent agent juggling the interests of her oddball clients, and a haunting memoir of growing up in suburban Orange County and coming of age in 1970s glitter-era Los Angeles.

Get Rich Quick
Peter Doyle
256 PAGES, HARDBACK, $22.95

"If Elmore Leonard came from down under, his name would be Peter Doyle."
—*KINKY FRIEDMAN*

Peter Doyle's novels brilliantly explore the criminal underworld, high-level political corruption, and postwar explosion of sex, drugs, and rock 'n' roll in 1950s Sydney. *Get Rich Quick*, winner of the Ned Kelly Award for Best First Crime Novel, introduces Doyle's irresistible hero, Billy Glasheen. Billy has a gift for masterminding elaborate scenarios—whether it's a gambling scam, transporting a fortune in stolen jewels, or keeping the wheels greased during the notorious 1957 tour by Little Richard and his rock 'n' roll entourage. But trouble follows close behind—perhaps because Billy's schemes always seem to interfere with the plans of Sydney's big players, an unholy trinity of crooks, bent cops, and politicians on the make.

Further information: www.versechorus.com / PO Box 14806, Portland OR 97293